Mean Mary Jean

Mean Mary Jean

Mary Jean Fielder

Black Belt Press

Montgomery

BLACK BELT PRESS
P.O. Box 551
Montgomery, AL 36101

A version of this book was published previously by SEVGO Press of
Northport, Alabama. The present edition has been edited and
contains new material.

Library of Congress Cataloging-in-Publication Data

Fielder, Mary Jean, 1945-
  Mean Mary Jean / Mary Jean Fielder.
      p.cm.
    ISBN 1-881320-51-0
    1. Fielder, Mary Jean, 1945–. 2.Tuscaloosa (Ala.)—Biography.
I. Title.
    CT275.f5514A3 1996
    976.1'063'092—dc20   96-23007
        [B]   CIP

 *The Black Belt, defined by its dark, rich soil, stretches across
central Alabama. It was the heart of the cotton belt. It was
and is a place of great beauty, of extreme wealth and grinding
poverty, of pain and joy. Here we take our stand, listening to
the past, looking to the future.*

To my grandmother,

WILLIE AVERY LEWIS FIKES

And her great-grandchildren

LANCE, COURTNEY, AND ASHLEY

CONTENTS

Teddy and Me

Past certain ages or certain wisdoms it is very difficult

to look with wonder; it is best done when one

is a child; after that, and if you are lucky,

you will find a bridge of childhood and walk across it.

—Truman Capote

ACKNOWLEDGMENTS

ON MY FIFTIETH birthday my brother said, "Only the good die young, so you're definitely no longer in danger." I suppose he's right, even though I remind him that at forty I won the jitterbug and twist contest at Yesterdays in Panama City, Florida. I guess I'm somehow trying to justify the age I feel inside.

My brother has watched me skip and stumble through life. I don't believe in divorce, but I've been divorced twice. Now, believing the third time's the charm, I am married again. I have birthed three babies and have acquired four stepsons. My children, despite my love for them, have helped me understand why some mothers in the animal kingdom eat their young. I have a precious granddaughter, Peyton, who is the promise of the adventures to come.

A special word to Sally Bean and Ronnie and Betty Rawlins who, for more than three decades, have saved my letters and urged me to write a book: Here it is, now may I please have my letters back!

I have been blessed by good friends. I list them all with affection, hoping they and their extended families will buy my book. These are long-suffering friends who gave me the gift of their time listening to my stories and rewrites. I consider myself fortunate to be able to thank them in print: Carolyn Platt, Richard and Brian Ensley, Millie Hawk, Rhonda Hobbs, Cindy Irvin, Mic Goodin, Wendy Brackin, Jackie Earnest, Lydall and Johnny Jones, Joe McClellen, Peggy Elliott, Sharon Bell, and my husband, Bob Fogal.

I am grateful to my friends in the Alabama Writer's Conclave, particularly Alabama's poet laureate, Helen Blackshear. They helped me turn a mass of scribbled-on legal pads into a book.

Mean Mary Jean

Parents sometimes find it hard to

hear what their children really

need—because their own childhood

still rings in their ears.

MEAN MARY JEAN

*B*EING CALLED "Mean Mary Jean" is not something I'm proud of. I wish I could say it was totally undeserved, but according to my Aunt Lou, I did commit the heinous crimes resulting in the label that has followed me through life.

Personally, I feel that I am innocent of all charges. The first offense I'm aware of only because my Aunt Lou repeated the story ad nauseam. I was only four and too young to even remember. According to her, one late afternoon I had some baby ducks in the watering trough up by the barn, watching them swim. Becoming bored with that, I placed several baby chickens in the water and derived much pleasure watching them flutter, sink, and die.

Now, since I can't remember doing this, I feel like it really didn't happen. But *if* it did, I have chosen to recreate my own scenario of that afternoon's activities.

It would seem only natural for such a young child to confuse little yellow chickens with little yellow ducks. And I do prefer to believe this was the case. When Mother called me to supper, the chickens looked like they were having so much fun I just couldn't bring myself to disturb them. As the story goes, Aunt Lou went up to the barn after supper and found the baby chickens weren't having fun any longer. From then on, she could be heard to say, "You know how mean Mary Jean is? She is so mean she drowns baby chickens."

THE SECOND crime was done with no malicious intent, just an immature thought process.

Some Sunday afternoons, we'd all get together at my Aunt Ethel and Uncle Ira's. They lived in a "section house" by the railroad tracks in Duncanville, Alabama. Off to the side of the house was an old barn with a corn crib. It goes without saying that old barns and corn cribs attract rats. In order to keep the rats at bay, Aunt Ethel kept cats around. At least one of those cats always had kittens. Kittens that upon seeing you either vanished in a flash or assumed the battle position: arched backs, hair standing on end, hissing, spitting, and bouncing around on their tiny, unbelievably sharp claws.

Behind the barn was a smokehouse filled with hanging carcasses of meat and large aluminum cans filled with lard. I spent many a Sunday afternoon drawing lard pictures in the top of those buckets. Using my dirty little hands to smooth the lard like a piece of white paper, I'd sit down and draw my pictures with a a small stick or a piece of pine straw. With the lard pictures finished, I'd tear out after the little wild kittens again.

One particular Sunday, after I had finished my pictures, I managed to catch a little calico kitten. It was so fuzzy. Just as I held it up to get a good look at its tiny face, I heard Mother calling, "Mary Jean, time to go."

Exasperatedly, I told the little kitten, "I just caught you, I wish I could put you someplace I could find you when I come back." Then I happened to think of the lard bucket.

I ran back into the smoke house and smooshed the kitten down in the lard with its little head sticking out and replaced the lid. You would get in trouble for leaving the top off of a lard bucket.

A few weeks later we all went back to Aunt Ethel's. Mama, Mom Boyd, Grannie Willie, and Aunt Lou were making fried apple pies. They had quite an assembly line going. Apparently, they ran low on shortening so Grandmother sent Aunt Lou, of all people, to the smokehouse to get some lard.

I had forgotten all about the kitten and was busy eating muscadines and catching tadpoles in the creek. My concentration was broken by a bloodcurdling cry from the smokehouse. Then it seemed as if everyone was calling my name. I threw down my jar of tadpoles and flew into the kitchen. Looking around, it was obvious that whatever had happened, I had done it. Aunt Lou was sitting slumped in a chair trying to tell what she had seen in the smokehouse. Grandmother was putting a cold rag on her forehead. I can't remember exactly what Mother said, but Aunt Ethel came to my defense saying it was her lard and her kitten and she didn't want to see me get a whippin'.

I had to sit on the front porch in a rocking chair all the rest of the afternoon. I don't remember understanding exactly what I had done.

Later on that afternoon, Aunt Lou came out on the porch and clamped her hand over my nose and mouth. When I started gasping for air, she said, "How do you think that poor little kitten felt being crammed down in that lard bucket in a dark place unable to breathe?"

The realization of what a horrible thing I had done was bad enough. But not as lasting as the effect of what Aunt Lou had done to me that afternoon on the porch. Many nights after that I remember waking up, in the dark . . . unable to breathe.

THUS BEGIN the tales of Mean Mary Jean.

BURLESS LOVES ME

*W*HEN I WAS born we lived at #6 Engleside Village in a tiny white house with the green-black shutters typical of the time. Next door lived my Great-uncle Loman and my Great-aunt Bertha. They had two children; Jerry, who was several years older than me, and Caroline, a few years younger. Beside them lived the Oilers, Joe and Jean, with their two sons, Burless and Winfred, and a daughter named Janice. My mother and Jean were good friends; they say Burless and I teethed on each other, but I only know that we were together from my earliest recollection.

Burless and I became engaged when we were about four and told our families we were getting married as soon as we grew up. Daddy and Joe laughed out loud, Mother and Jean smiled. We were relieved our decision had made them so happy. Sometimes at our age it was hard to know which things to tell and which to keep secret.

Both our fathers could be harsh, but after a few Pabst Blue Ribbons Burless's father was definitely the most fun. He said

Mama, Me, Daddy

since Burless and I were getting married we should learn how to dance together. He taught us to waltz to Hank Williams singing the *Tennessee Waltz*. He taught us how to hold each other in dance position and at first would repeat, "One-two-three, one-two-three," until we could float around the living room without his cadence. He would sing along with Hank as Burless and I continued the dance.

Burless and I, as do most young people in love, suffered interference, mostly at the hands of my cousin Jerry from next door. Jerry would sit on his back steps eating a disgusting sandwich of peanut butter, bananas, and mayonnaise while he pitted us against each other. He would say, "Burless, Mary Jean said she could beat you up." And while Burless ran home to look for a weapon, he would tell me, "Burless said he could beat you up," then quietly take a seat on the back steps and wait. Burless would appear to Jerry's left with his weapon, usually a two-by-four so big he could hardly drag it, and I would be at the right of the yard piling up rocks. As we eyed one another the tirade of normal four-year-old verbal repartee would occur — "Oh yeah?" "Oh yeah" — and end with — "My daddy can beat up your daddy."

Then I *had* to fight. Burless and I were an even match, but Joe Oiler would have made two of my daddy. As a little person, even if you know it's true, hollering back, "Oh yeah? I *know* your daddy can beat mine up," is just too humiliating. The fight would commence. Hitting, biting, scratching, crying, and sometimes bleeding, we would go at each other.

Aunt Bertha would run out the screen door and see Burless and me thrashing around in the dirt and call our mothers. Jerry would still be sitting on the steps with his hands folded angelically as he tried to hide his satisfaction over the entertainment he had directed.

Mother and Jean would pull us apart still kicking and swinging at each other. Then we'd have to hug each other. After all the energy and anger were released, we were both relieved to be friends again. Mother and Jean would go a step further telling us we couldn't play together and then take us in opposite directions to our respective houses, crying because we were being separated.

One morning playing cowboys, I got wounded. Boys didn't get wounded as often as girls did so we proceeded from cowboys to doctor in a rather orderly fashion. I don't remember playing doctor after that initial discovery, but I do remember being sad and disappointed that we were different.

Another day we decided to play barber shop behind the hedge in the Oilers' front yard. I sent Burless in to get his mother's scissors and proceeded to remove every natural curl off his baby sister's golden head. Unfortunately for Burless and Winfred, Joe Oiler came into our barber shop that day. Burless, as much as he loved me, denied doing the cutting, but he got a terrible licking for getting me the scissors and not protecting his sister. Poor

Winfred got a whipping just for watching. I ran home.

A couple of days later Mother saw Janice's hair, or lack thereof. She inquired as to the choice of Janice's rather unusual hairstyle. Jean told her it wasn't exactly *their* choice. Mother wasn't angry; she was frothing mad: mad because I did it and mad because I hadn't gotten my comeuppance when Burless did. And she was terribly embarrassed. A frothing mad, embarrassed woman can be nearly lethal with something as simple as a switch.

Now, this wasn't fair. If Mother *hadn't* asked, Jean wouldn't have told on me! Mother didn't tattle on Burless, that way we didn't get in trouble quite as much, and furthermore, this happened two or three days ago and *that* was a really long time.

ONE HOUSE down from Burless was a tiny public park. One day Burless and I had a little spat, he shoved me, and I fell into a small ditch. The middle of my foot landed on a broken Coke bottle. Burless ran for help. Daddy carried me to old Doc Oliver's next to the Yellow Front store. A lot of people held me down as they placed five metal clamps across the arch of my foot. I remember Burless standing up by my head with tears rolling from his eyes saying, "I'm sorry, I'm sorry, I'm never gonna let them put clamps in *my* foot." Dr. Oliver said I had to stay off my foot for at least *three weeks*.

After a few days, I persuaded Mother to let me up and out by proving to her I could walk on my hands and one foot with my sore foot stuck up in the air like an antenna. Burless walked the same way so I wouldn't look so funny. One thing about Burless, he'd never run off and leave you like the big kids did.

When we were five, my family built a house out on my granddaddy's farm because they decided the city was not a proper place to raise children.

Burless and I cried the whole afternoon as they packed our things. Not long after that Burless's family moved to Mississippi, and they stopped by the farm to tell us good-by.

Burless and I renewed our vows to each other and stuck a pin in our pointer fingers to symbolize our union as blood brothers, and he said one day he'd come back for me.

We never wrote, I guess in the beginning because we didn't know how, but our mothers did occasionally.

When my mom was fatally injured in a car crash, Burless, his mother, and Winfred came. It had been thirteen years since Burless and I had seen each other. I introduced him to the man at my side, my future husband, and he and Burless shook hands.

As they left, Burless hugged me and said softly, "I'll always love you, Mary Jean." He turned away quickly not waving or looking back. Tears rained down my cheeks as I watched him drive away.

I realized the innocence of my childhood had left with him.

MRS. SMITH AND THE HONEYBEES

WHEN I WAS little, I had a very special place where I was always welcome. My great-grandmother, Mom Boyd, lived in a small house between my grandfather's house and ours. When I would get in trouble I'd make a "bee line" for Mom Boyd's. I would barrel in crying and lay my head in her lap, and between sobs, tell her how mean everybody was to me. She would rub my stringy blond hair back away from my wet eyes and tell me that Mama and Grandmother were so busy they had just forgotten what it was like to be little and that she knew they realized how precious I was. She always made me feel better.

After she died, Granddaddy rented her little house to the Smiths. I hated having somebody else living in Mom Boyd's house, and I guess that's why I developed an immediate dislike for Mrs. Smith and her children, Jo Ann, Linda Fay, and Ruby Neil.

I aggravated Mrs. Smith so much she forbade me to even walk through her yard. So I would sit on the terrace in the red-topped clover between the two houses and catch honey bees in a fruit jar while I made up ugly songs about her and sang them at the top of my lungs.

Watching the honey bees, I found out that after they landed on a blossom of clover there was a split second when their wings would stop flapping as they sucked out the nectar. During that split second I could grab their wings between my thumb and forefinger. In that position they couldn't sting me, and I'd drop them down in a jar.

One afternoon I had taken up my usual position in the clover to catch bees and sing hateful songs, when I thought up what I perceived to be my very best song. It was to the tune of "It's Howdy Doody Time," and to this day I can remember the words:

> It's Neil Smith's time
> She isn't worth a dime,
> She smells like turpentine
> *and looks like Frankenstein.*

Over and over I sang my song until Mrs. Smith came out. She didn't send Jo Ann, Ruby Neil, or Linda Fay out to chase me off and she didn't holler at me the way she usually did. She just smiled and walked slowly toward me and said in a sweet voice, "I've been watching you catch those honey bees from the kitchen window. I've got a trick I can show you where you can catch a bunch of 'em at one time."

"You do?" I said.

"Yes. You find several of them together and clap your hands on them, and it will stun them for a few seconds while you put 'em in the jar."

She was so nice. She sat down and helped me watch the clover until about six bees lit real close together and she said, "Now, clap your hands real quick!"

I did.

Then I looked up at her and said, "I have to go home now." I picked up my fruit jar and waited till I got behind the hedges in my yard to look at my hands and cry. I would have died before I let her see how much she hurt me.

But I'll tell you something: Neil Smith taught me a very valuable lesson. When somebody you've been mean to smiles at you, you better take your bees and run!

Please Don't Take my Mama—I'll Never Call the Police Again

*W*HEN I WAS in first grade, Mother went to work for a nearby landscaping company. I hated it. She had always been at home. Now when I came in from school, I was greeted by eerie silence. I was supposed to come home, put up my things, and join my brother and sister next door at Grandmother's. Instead, I would run in, throw my things down, and call Mother at work. She had told me repeatedly not to call her at the office unless it was an emergency. So every afternoon I created one. While never actually lying, I did exaggerate everything to crisis proportions so they would constitute an emergency. Every afternoon I called Mother and frightened her half out of her wits. Sometimes I would upset her so badly she'd leave work and come flying home.

One afternoon while getting off the bus, I noticed a big white cat lying in the front yard. I got a peach basket from the barn and placed it over the sleeping cat. Suddenly, remembering all the excitement of a few months back when the Smith's hound dog got rabies, I decided the cat must have the same affliction. I called the police and told them there was a cat with rabies in my front yard under a peach basket and they should come right away. Then I called my mother and told her not to worry, everything was under control, and the police were on their way. I hung up knowing she'd be proud.

Shortly thereafter, Mother wheeled into the driveway. She marched straight to the ligustrum bush, broke off a switch, and charged in through the front door. As she nettled my legs, she began to cry, "If the police do come all the way out here, it won't be to get a cat. They will be coming to get me." She sent me to my room. I knelt by the side of my bed, folded my hands, and began to pray, "Please, God, don't let the police take my mother away." I stayed on my knees in my room until it was dark, pleading with God.

Then Daddy came home. I figured, if Daddy's office was closed, the police office must be closed too and Mother was safe!

I thanked God for not letting them take Mother away and promised Him *never* to call the police again . . . without a really good reason.

How To Get Expelled
Without Really Trying

MAYBE I WAS angry at Mother for working. Maybe I didn't want a brother or sister. At six and a half, what do you really know? I can't believe I consciously set out to get expelled from second grade.

The old plank school house was built up on concrete blocks, and we little ones could stand straight up and walk under it. Some of the boys had been playing Indians all week, laying pebbles around make-believe campfires and hopping up and down, popping their lips with the palms of their hands and making Indian noises.

The roof of my teepee was actually the floor to the school. There were matches on Mrs. Garrison's desk. She used them to light the old wood stove in our classroom, and it really *was* cold that day. I'll always believe it was Mary Evelyn Neighbors that ran for Mrs. Spiller, the principal, because she got so upset when I lit the matches in my teepee.

The end of my tenure at Taylorville Elementary came a month or so later. Grandmother had given me a paper sack of pecans to give to our school bus driver, Mr. Coleburn. I always waited for the bus by the highway in a huge field of red-topped clover. I was the last child they picked up, so I would amuse myself by catching honeybees by their wings with my thumb and forefinger. I was really good at it. Naturally I just dropped them down in the paper sack with the pecans. I had caught several dozen bees by the time my old yellow bus number 77 arrived. I climbed the big steps into the bus and handed the sack to Mr. Coleburn. "Grandmother sent you this," I said. While he opened the sack, I skipped to the back of the bus.

Children were screaming, the ones that got stung were crying, and Mr. Coleburn was opening the windows, getting everybody out of the bus. He got stung on the forehead twice, but I didn't get stung.

I did, however, get expelled from the public school system of the state of Alabama.

THE EYES OF JESUS ARE UPON YOU

IN 1952 MY mother had a four-year-old daughter and a two-year-old son, besides being blessed with me, and by the time I got expelled from the second grade, she had endured more than most mothers endure in a lifetime. Her family had, for as far back as we know, been Baptist, but Mother was desperate. I remember being taken by the hand and delivered to Sister Mary Barbara, principal of St. Johns Catholic Elementary School in Tuscaloosa. I was absolutely terrified. All I knew about nuns was that Sara Elizabeth Hinton had told me they were witches, wore long black robes, and shaved their heads. But my teacher, Sister Marie Antoinette, seemed less ominous. She had a kind face, what I could see of it, and looked a little bit like my Grandmother. She showed me to a seat, gave me my books, and said I would address her as "Sister."

"Yes, ma'am," I said.

"No," she said. "'Yes, Sister.'"

"Yes, Sister." Yes, ma'am and No, ma'am were replaced with Yes, Sister and No, Sister. Remembering it was a different story.

School Days
1951 - 1952

SCHOOL DAYS
1952 - 1953

SCHOOL DAYS
1956 - 1957

SCHOOL DAYS 1959 -'60
Tuscaloosa High

SCHOOL DAYS
1953 - 1954

SCHOOL DAYS
1955 - 1956

These people prayed all the time: 8:00 a.m. in church at Mass until 8:30, then to the classroom, pray before you start the day, pray before recess, after recess, before lunch, after lunch, even before we went home. They taught us prayers to say when we went to bed at night and when we got up in the morning.

My entire body, all forty-eight pounds of it, suffered a major overload: no running in the halls, no breaking in line, no talking, never talking back, speaking only when spoken to, and remembering, "Yes, Sister."

I was given much more to remember than I could possibly comprehend. For example, I found out quickly that when I talked back, I got pinched on the arm, and then sent to Sister Barbara.

It was really difficult not to take up for myself or use some kind of excuse. They even tried to teach me to tell on myself! The other children had been brainwashed. Sister would say, "Who did it?" and they would stand up and confess. At first I tried just taking my chances if I had done the offense in question, but I soon learned the other children, honor bound, would tell on me.

I had been there three days in Sister Marie Antoinette's class, watching her every move as her habit, the long black veil, swayed as she walked. I kept wondering if Sara Elizabeth was right and if she did, in fact, have a shaved head. When Sister walked by my desk I would lean over in vain to get a peek under the back of her habit, all the while imagining her bald head. I guess, because she was so hard of hearing, I decided that her other senses might also be dulled, so I took hold of the end of her habit to lift it up. Unfortunately, she could still feel and jerked her head around in my direction, leaving me sitting there holding the long, black veil.

Nuns are very strange when it comes to their attire, which they think of as holy articles to be revered, not snatched off by curious little girls. She gasped and screamed for Sister Barbara, and I was escorted to the community room. It was a room with a long, shiny table and about ten chairs, a crucifix on one wall, and, at the very end of the room, a large picture of Jesus.

I sat at the table for what seemed like an eternity, and finally the door opened. In walked Sister Barbara, accompanied by my mother and father. I still get goose bumps when I think of the looks on their faces. Sister Barbara had summoned them both from work.

They talked, Mother cried, I was very quiet. They seemed to think that I had snatched Sister Marie Antoinette's habit off out of hatefulness and disrespect. I was too frightened to defend myself. I guess I figured telling them that I just wanted to see if she had hair would somehow have made things worse. After my mother's pleadings and my father's giving his permission to take whatever steps necessary to control me, *they left me there* with Sister Barbara.

I DIDN'T GET much of a chance to make friends that year because we weren't allowed to talk in class and I no longer had the privilege of recess. My recesses for the remainder of the third grade were spent in the community room, just me, sitting in one of the big chairs at the long table with only the crucifix and the picture of Jesus at the end of the room.

Besides school work, I had punishments to do every day. I wrote "lines," as Sister Barbara called them, sometimes only fifty and sometimes as many as five hundred.

I will obey. I will not talk back. I will not run in the halls. I will not be disrespectful. I will not, I will not, I will not.

I tried making a game out of the lines, seeing how many pencils I could weave between my fingers to write two, three or even four lines at the same time. But I was constantly vexed by an eerie feeling that someone was watching me.

I would look up, and the eyes of Jesus in the picture would be staring straight at me. No matter where I sat, they were always looking at me. I would move from one big chair to another, from the head of the table down to the end, but the eyes would follow.

One day I got *under* the table to do my lines, hoping He couldn't see me there, but when I peeked out, He was still watching.

After nearly a year of confinement, I had a startling revelation — no matter what I did, even outside of the community room, the eyes of Jesus would always be upon me.

By the way, Sister Marie Antoinette had long, gray hair, swept up in a tight bun at the nape of her neck.

Green Apples and Polio

ONE LATE afternoon I was enjoying myself doing two things at the same time that I'd been told not to do. I was perched in the top of Granddaddy's apple tree that he told me not to climb, eating green apples Mama told me not to eat.

It was hard being a kid with so many relatives living near by. They each had their own different set of rules that I was supposed to remember and obey. Too many rules for a six-year-old, so I did what I felt like doing and suffered the consequences.

Mama hollered for me to come in to supper. The sound of her voice pierced my tranquillity, and I dropped my apple and fell out of the tree. On the way down, the branches scraped the backs of my legs. I got up, wiped my tears, brushed myself off, and went to supper.

That night, I took my bath and put on a long gown to hide the evidence from Mama. But during the night, I became very ill. I was so sick at my stomach. About midnight Mama was really getting concerned, so she called Aunt Lou from next door.

They took my temperature and felt my head and tried to

make me more comfortable as I winced in pain. Mama asked me if I hurt anywhere besides my stomach. Well, I did and I told her my legs hurt. She pulled away the covers and mashed on my legs, but she didn't see the scratches because they were on the back, and the few little bruises on the front were just part of how I usually looked. She didn't ask me if I knew why they hurt because I was just a child, and she and Aunt Lou had already decided I probably had polio.

Mama called Dr. Jackson in town and told him we had an emergency and that he better come right out. Dr. Jackson had delivered me and, to my knowledge, had always been our family doctor. He got there about 2:00 a.m. and sat on my bed and began checking and mashing on me.

But he was more thorough than Mama was and he noticed the scratches on the backs of my legs.

He asked Mama and Aunt Lou to wait outside, and he closed the door. Then he asked me how I got the scratches. I peeked around him to make sure the door was shut tightly and I whispered, "I fell out of a tree."

He looked at me for a second and asked the most amazing question. He asked me if, by chance, the tree I had fallen out of was an apple tree.

"Why, yes!" I exclaimed. He was such a smart man. I couldn't believe he could tell just from the scratches what kind of tree it was.

He patted me on the head and told me he'd leave some medicine with Mama, and that he was sure I'd be just fine by morning. Little did he realize what the rest of my morning would bring.

I didn't know what polio was at the time, but I was sure I would have preferred it to what followed . . .

We went to a new doctor after that, Dr. Tyler. Mama said she was too embarrassed to go back to Dr. Jackson.

And my granddaddy cut down the apple tree. I guess he wanted to make sure that none of us kids ever got exposed to polio again.

MALARIA AND MISCHIEF

MY GREAT-AUNT Essie had five brothers and two sisters. All of them smoked, dipped, or chewed. These habits were taken up when they were all quite young, kind of like a family tradition. Her father, Paw Fikes, chewed tobacco and her mother, Maw Fikes, dipped snuff.

One afternoon, Aunt Essie got a bright idea for an eleven-year-old; armed with a plug of tobacco, a can of Garrett's Snuff, and a pack of unfiltered cigarettes, she decided to see which one appealed to her the most. She slipped off behind a big stump at the back of the chicken yard and she proceeded to experience The World of Nicotine. After smoking several cigarettes and spittin' and swallowing the snuff, she bit off a big chaw of tobacco. Shortly thereafter, she passed out cold.

When she awoke, she could barely drag herself toward the house. Her mother noticed her trying to crawl up the back steps and ran to her screaming, "Essie what's the matter?"

Aunt Essie feebly answered, "I'm dying, Maw."

Maw Fikes yelled to the barn for her son, "Troy, get the

mule, ride to Hagler as fast as you can, and fetch old Doc Owens!"

When Troy returned with Doc Owens, they found Paw and Maw Fikes at the bedside of a very ashen-faced little girl. After examining, checking and rechecking, he made his diagnosis: Aunt Essie had a severe case of malaria.

Even though she was only eleven, Aunt Essie realized she did not have malaria. She knew she was suffering an affliction caused by her decision-making process.

Three weeks later, having been severely warned by her worried parents to take it easy so as not to bring on another attack, a rather shaky little girl emerged from her bed. She had been bedridden, not only from the massive dose of nicotine, but also because of the medication prescribed by Doc Owens. The quinine was bad enough, but the tonic, a thick yellowish concoction called Triple Six, nearly did her in.

Maw Fikes went to her grave eternally grateful to Doc Owens for so completely curing her daughter of "malaria."

For years, this deception tormented Aunt Essie. As big a stinker as she was, Aunt Essie did have a conscience. When she realized her father was dying, she could withhold the truth no longer. She pulled her chair up next to his bed and quietly whispered her confession.

Opening his eyes, Paw Fikes spoke his last words to his daughter, "Essie Bell, if I wasn't busy dying, I'd get up from this bed and beat you within an inch of your life."

A REMEDY FOR MARY JEAN

*L*OOKING BACK, I remember only one thing my entire family agreed on: I was too skinny, and something had to be done about it. Never before or since have I seen such a unified effort to achieve one common goal.

My appearance seemed to be a distraction from whatever else was bothering them. They clucked around me like large Rhode Island Reds wondering how this bantam biddy had come amongst them. Not only was I skinny, but also small-boned and short. They pointed out that even my hair was thin.

My birth weight was six pounds, two ounces; not really so tiny, but then I was also twenty-one inches long. They say my mother cried when she saw me and said there must have been some mistake. I was very red, with long arms and legs, and wild, fine hair that grew in no specific direction. Mother said I looked like a spider monkey. My grandfather was horrified when they brought me home, but his solution was simple—keep me in long dresses and long sleeves and when they fattened me up, I would look more human.

Now, I was born before anyone had heard of Twiggy. Thin wasn't in. Not only that — I was hyperkinetic and hypoglycemic long before these conditions came into fashion. Back then, a hyperactive child was simply labeled "bad." Their behavior was called "bouncing off the walls," and the cure was stricter discipline. Because of my activity level, I was never still long enough for the pounds to get a firm hold. The baby formula of the time was Carnation evaporated milk with Karo syrup added according to your weight gain. No weight gain, more Karo. When this failed, they tried buttermilk and finally goat's milk. This went on until I had the presence of mind to shove them away and scream if they brought anything white toward me.

So I went to table food. Grandmother saucer-cooled my coffee for breakfast, and I had tea for lunch and supper. Decaf was not an option at the time. I began to experience the effects of caffeine on my hyperactivity.

Mother, bless her, made weekly visits to Southside Drugstore to keep a check on the latest over-the-counter miracle drugs. In addition to vitamins and cod liver oil, she purchased Hadacol and Geritol in the giant economy size.

The tonic Nervine appeared in the late forties, and Mother decided that since my hands shook and I couldn't sit still, I had bad nerves. She gave me Nervine when my hands shook or when she was nervous, and a big dose at bedtime to insure a good night's sleep.

Because of its high alcohol content, Nervine did serve this purpose, but coupled with the same ingredient in my other tonics, I was undoubtedly in a drunken stupor for most of my formative years.

To top it off, after seeing beer-bellies on people who drank too much, my Aunt Lou convinced my mother to try giving me a can of beer with an SSS gelcap after supper.

Grandmother decided I should have a mid-morning and mid-afternoon snack, so she made me a shake from Ovaltine, malt, and milk. Now, that wasn't so terrible until Mom Boyd suggested adding two raw eggs.

I can't remember who was responsible for the Weight-On wafers, but apparently they saw the ad where the skinny little guy is laying on the beach and a muscular bully kicks sand in his face; then, the skinny guy eats Weight-On wafers and ta-ta, ta-ta — he turns into the Hulk. Well, I didn't turn into the Hulk, or gain any weight, but I do think I know what dog biscuits taste like.

My father took the psychological approach. He called me "bean pole," told me not to drink red Kool-Aid or I'd be mistaken for a thermometer, and not to stick out my lip when I pouted or people would think I was a zipper.

Even though I remain the smallest member of my family, their efforts were not without some merit. I have absolutely no taste or tolerance for alcohol, and I am blessed with an unbelievable instinct for survival.

Stories for Darlin'

CHILDREN SHOULD be seen and not heard. It was repeated to me often enough. But I guess I thought that if people didn't hear you, they didn't see you either. At supper, most of the time we'd be sitting around quietly. Daddy had worked all day and just wanted to eat in peace. Mother, too, had come in from work, cooked our supper, attended our needs, and as tired as she was already still had miles to go.

My little brother was developing a disgusting sense of humor. Bodily functions seemed to cut through the silence as he attempted his brand of entertainment. He'd make out like incidences such as burping were accidental and came in threes, the loudest usually first. Mother would gasp. Then he would act even more heathen and say loudly, "'Scuse me, I belched," instead of just "Pardon me," as she had taught us. The reason that he wasn't snatched from the table and delivered a sound switching was Mother knew exactly who had taught him by the age of three some rather undignified behavior.

Granddaddy never looked up, but Mother and I understood. My brother was under my Grandfather's protection. I heard him tell my brother one day, "No need to run all the way to the house, son, your Grandmother's chrysanthemums needed watering anyway."

Other than my Grandfather's strange idea of humor and my brother's misguided direction, the rest of the family seemed quite devoid of dinnertime entertainment. So I figured, since everybody was gathered all around, I would tell my stories. They would listen, even laugh sometimes. Now these weren't elaborate tales, just what had caught my attention that day. But I ran into a problem. My sister, Marie, my Mother's darlin', had been born with a slight birth defect, long since healed, but Mother had somehow accepted the guilt for her imperfection and had granted her special status. Marie was appalled at my having everybody's attention, especially Mother's, and would attempt to edit my reports. I will admit a few times I did put a little lace on the muslin, but for the most part, the gist of what I was telling was the God's truth.

When I would begin to tell a story I'd say, "It happened just about dark." Marie'd say, "It was not, it was this mornin'."

I'd say, "We were all out in the back yard."

"Were not, we were out in the front."

I'd say, "It was a black, wolflike dog."

"Was not. It was the Smith's spotted hound."

"A storm was comin' up."

"The sun was shinin'."

I'd nudge her gently under the table with my foot, realizing I was losing my audience's attention. They were becoming bored and aggravated, never finding out what I was trying to tell them because my sister and I couldn't agree on the more trivial details.

"You just exaggerate everything," she'd say. As I changed my nudge to a gentle kick, sometimes we'd begin telling the two stories at the same time. Mother would have enough, shush us both, telling us to just be quiet and finish our dinner. Angrily, I'd study my plate, wanting to flick a forkful of whatever across the dinner table.

On extremely frustrating occasions, if I thought an especially tantalizing tale had been ruined, I'd give her another not-so-gentle kick under the table, at which time my sister could wail like I'd cut off both her arms and left her in a ditch to die. More often than not, my stories were interrupted by a switching or going to bed without finishing supper.

As little children, my sister and I didn't understand it was my calling to tell the stories, just as it was hers to be Mama's Darlin'.

Me, Mama, Marie

Jimmy's Chicken

SIBLING RELATIONSHIPS are all so different and complex. Everyone who saw my two precious towheaded little boys would say how wonderful for us that since they were only twenty-one months apart they would be such good friends. Observers always see things as they aren't. The day I brought Courtney home from the hospital, I overheard Lance asking the mailman if he wanted a baby. He proceeded to tell him we had one, but we didn't want it. This set the tone for the next fourteen years.

When they were small, Courtney would say, "You love Lance more than you do me. You gave him the most juice." Trying hard to be a good mother, not favoring one child over the other, I would carefully measure juice to the silly millimeter. I cut cakes and pies with the precision of a surgeon. At one point, I purchased glasses they couldn't see through. So, they stood on their chairs and peered into the liquid, admonishing me tearfully for my unfairness.

They nearly killed each other biting, hitting, scratching,

fighting and running to me for justice. Finally they reached a point where they had gotten so big they stopped the fighting. Loving each other seemed preferable to being mortally wounded. Also, they had a common bond — the anger they felt for the person punishing them, whom they were convinced didn't understand how to administer justice.

Later, even when I was aware of exactly what was going on, I would let it slide because they were covering up for each other. I much preferred that they had come through their battle as friends and co-conspirators in crime. They seemed to have learned it was okay not to like each other all the time because they realized they really loved each other.

Unfortunately, my sister Marie and I never reached this point of friendship or unconditional love. There was a four-year difference in our ages. Marie was younger, and I felt she spent the majority of her formative years tattling and looking for ways to bring punishment upon me. Since she was no match in a fair fight, she devised ways to get me into trouble.

When one of us did something wrong, Mom would ask, "Who did it?" If the guilty one did not confess, then she would whip us both. She justified this by saying if we weren't the guilty party we could accept the spanking for some earlier crime we thought we had gotten away with. *This* made perfect sense to Mother. However, when it got to the point of the punishment being delivered and I was the culprit, I would confess in order to spare Marie a punishment she didn't deserve. My sister, however, did not reciprocate. If she were guilty, she would take her punishment happily, while I suffered unjustly through mine, and she would smile at me as mother left the room. Sometimes my anger would explode, and I would stupidly attack her before mother was out of earshot.

One Easter, we all got baby chickens. Marie got a pink one, I got a blue one and my baby brother Jim's was green. Marie and I literally loved ours to death, but Jim's survived to be a big, white hen with the green paint of its youth tinting its feathers. It was always with us outside. I don't remember its having a name other than Jimmy's chicken.

A bunch of us were playing tackle football in the back yard one afternoon and the big, white chicken was with us as usual. It ran up and down the field as we raced from goal to goal. Somehow during the game at about mid-field, the chicken managed to get caught in a big pile of arms and legs. As we untangled, the chicken began flopping around the yard — its neck broken. Children ran screaming and crying in all directions.

Marie wasn't even playing that day. But, even now, thirty-three years later, if she heard me repeat this story, she'd still say Jimmy's chicken was *blue*. Sometimes sibling rivalry never ends.

I love my sister. I only wish that over the years, our relationship could have progressed to the point where the color of Jimmy's chicken just didn't matter anymore.

Teddy and Jimmy

Aunt Lou

A CHILD OF HER OWN

AFTER SEVERAL miscarriages, Aunt Lou was told by her doctor that she would never have a child. She wasn't the same after that. It was as if she set out on a mission to prove she never wanted children anyway. With unconscious wisdom, I decided to prove to her she was right, even though she was the one who called me "Mean Mary Jean."

To help her, I felt compelled to spend the night with her on occasion. It was easy for me to get her upset with something as simple as jumping out of the tub on her fluffy mats without drying off. She had the most wonderful assortment of perfumes and nail polishes on her dresser, and she could tell if you picked one up, even if you put it right back where you got it. The mysterious white marks fingernail polish remover would leave on her cherry vanity could take her mind off her problem for days. After one of these episodes, she would wake me up early and take me home, and Mother would give me a talk about respecting other people's property.

She loved her flowers, so I would pick them and bring them

to her. I climbed her trees, jumped on the bed, spilt stuff, and tracked mud on her clean floors. It seemed like I didn't have to try very hard to give her other things to think about. Yet after all the things I did, I still thought she loved me.

Aunt Lou and I would go downtown and spend whole days together. We would get our hair done at the beauty shop where she took me for my first manicure. She would take me to H&W Drugs for a chocolate malt, and afterwards we would go to the movies. We looked so much alike, people often asked if I was her daughter. Aunt Lou would look at me so sadly and say in a gruff voice, "She should have been."

As she got older, she never felt good anymore. She was always coming down with something. She said my presence brought on a migraine. When I was sixteen, I drove her everywhere because she was too nervous to drive. She would slam on imaginary brakes and occasionally cover her face from impending crashes that never occurred. She would fuss at me to turn the radio off so I could concentrate.

When she was sixty-seven, she finally got a real disease, cancer, and she suffered terribly. She was so angry and afraid. The last time she went to the hospital she called and asked me to come stay with her. I was holding her hand as she drew her last breath. I just sat there for a while and wondered how much it had really mattered that I wasn't a child of her own.

Finally, I folded Aunt Lou's hands and rang for the nurse.

UNCLE RIP

WILLARD WAS his given name, but Rip suited him because he ripped apart everything he came in contact with, including my Aunt Lou's heart.

Uncle Rip served in World War II and received not only the purple heart but also the silver star. I know all about these things because Aunt Lou used them as an excuse for his alcoholism. In my mind, there was no excuse for the things he continually did.

Aunt Lou would send us a picture of their new car and descriptions of the absolute "doll houses" she could make out of the old trailers and houses they lived in. But soon after, the car would be wrecked, the houses destroyed, and Uncle Rip would be back in the hospital or jail. Aunt Lou would be working two jobs to pay his doctor bills or make his bail.

I remember being with her one night when we found his car down a gully in some kudzu. He was lying on the ground half frozen and drunk. As usual he survived, but Aunt Lou died a little.

Once when he was on the wagon, I rode the bus to Aunt Lou's in Demopolis for a week's visit all by myself. I felt so grown up. The next afternoon, Aunt Lou and I walked to the movies. I don't remember what we saw, but the walk I still vividly remember. We went down the sidewalk past antebellum homes fronted by immaculate lawns with azaleas and daffodils shaded by blooming dogwoods. We walked all the way to the river. I was sorry when we had to go home.

After we fixed supper, Aunt Lou watched the clock. The ticking seemed so loud despite the noise of the rain outside. It was beginning to storm. Finally, we ate without Uncle Rip, and I went to bed. When I awoke later that night, I thought I'd been having a nightmare, but it was Uncle Rip. He was staggering around, ranting and raving. He took all our clothes and threw them over the balcony into the mud puddles below. Aunt Lou and I slipped out the next morning and took the bus home. She didn't mention what had happened the night before.

As usual, she didn't stay long. Sometimes Uncle Rip would show up with flowers. Other times he would stand outside the house bellowing what he called Aunt Lou when he was drunk — *Lou lee bell, Lou lee bell* — like a mooing cow. My mother seemed to be the only one who could quiet him down and make him go away. Sometimes she shamed him; other times she reminded him Granddaddy was just down the hill.

Once before, Uncle Rip had awakened him. Granddaddy had grabbed his 12-gauge and charged up to the house. Mother and Aunt Lou managed somehow to stop Granddaddy that night. Perched on the window sill in my room, I was waiting to watch him shoot Uncle Rip. I was so surprised when Granddaddy handed the gun to my mother. He doubled up his big fists, glaring at Uncle Rip. Then he told him to get off his land and never cause another ruckus, or he'd think he'd been sleeping with a circular saw. Uncle Rip left.

Another time when he was "on a tear," as Grandmother politely called a binge, he slipped in the back door looking for Aunt Lou. He staggered into my room and said, "Give your old uncle Rip a kiss." I couldn't have been more than six, but I wasn't having any of it. I beaned him with a big jar of Lady Astor cold cream. He fell over, and everybody thought he'd hit his head on the dresser. Of course, he couldn't remember.

One night a few weeks later, Mother woke us up in the middle of the night. We drove to Childersburg to get Aunt Lou. Uncle Rip's latest job was there at the mill. Daddy went into the house and brought her out. Her hand was bandaged. She had somehow badly burned it on an eye of the stove.

It seemed like every time Aunt Lou had some small glimmer of happiness, Uncle Rip was there to squelch it. I couldn't believe how forgiving Aunt Lou and Mother were. I certainly wasn't.

One afternoon he had promised to take Aunt Lou and me out to dinner. Even though he had recently joined Alcoholics Anonymous, Uncle Rip had already had a few when we left. As always, Aunt Lou made out like nothing was wrong, I guess thinking I was too young to know the difference; but I knew.

That night he drove us to a seafood house on the river. He slammed on the brakes when he parked and left the front bumper hanging over the ledge with the river rippling so far below in the dark. This time he scared me really bad! We went inside to sit down. Aunt Lou and I ate as he drank. He could barely walk when we left the restaurant. Aunt Lou pretended things were fine and remarked how beautiful the big white blooms were on the lily pads in the water. He started staggering out into the river, telling Aunt Lou he was going to get her some of the pretty flowers. He was out in the water almost to his waist, and Aunt Lou was running around the edge of the bank pleading with him to please come out.

The current grew much swifter not far beyond where Uncle Rip was standing. I yelled to him, "The flowers further out are the prettiest." Aunt Lou grabbed me by my shoulders and shook me saying, "What are you trying to do? Do you want him to drown?" I lowered my head. I hadn't thought about his drowning. I only wanted the water to wash him away and carry him out of my Aunt Lou's life and mine.

Two Doses of Meanness

WHEN MY grandfather, David Troy Fikes, made decisions, they stayed made. He was a big man with a big voice, and it was said behind his back that he was hardheaded as a goat. I never saw many people try to take exception to him, and the ones that did wished they hadn't. Granddaddy ruled his land like the Don Corleone of Taylorville.

I wasn't sure rules were a good thing back then. Some I simply ignored until I got caught. Rules like no fishing on Sunday just seemed stupid to me, so I kept a cane pole hidden by the spring and a fruit jar to keep bait in. One particular Sunday, Granddaddy caught me, pole in hand sitting at the pond. "What do you think you are doing? How many times do you think I'm going to tell you, the Bible says Sunday is a day of rest. And that means *no fishing*."

Of course I didn't say it, but I was thinking if God hadn't wanted me fishing it wouldn't be such a pretty day and the fish wouldn't be biting. We had the neatest fish pond, and most Sunday afternoons were just perfect for fishing. I got so mad at him. I knew there would be no discussion, and his mind was made up. Since I couldn't talk to him, I wouldn't look at him either.

"Look at me when I talk to you, girl!" For some reason when he forgot my name, I did have the good sense to take a more humble demeanor.

After Granddaddy went back in the house, I started kicking rocks and muttering about no fishin' and his being so mean. Then I began to cry. This was not something I, Mean Mary Jean, did very often and I certainly wouldn't let anybody see me. But Uncle Charlie had. He called me over to the swing and took me up in his lap. I threw my arms around his neck deciding, since he'd already seen me crying, I might as well have a good one.

Uncle Charlie was one of my favorites. Every time he came to visit, he would grab me up, give me a big hug, slip a dime in my hand and say, "That's my pretty girl!" It was different when he called me "girl." I always thought he would have made a great father. I asked grandmother one day why he and Aunt Edna didn't have any children. She said, "The mumps went down on him." Then she turned away. I didn't know where the mumps went, but I knew Grandmother had said her piece on the subject.

"Uncle Charlie," I said, "how come you and Granddaddy are brothers, and you are always so sweet and he's so mean?" Looking at me, he gave me his handkerchief and told me to wipe my eyes and blow my nose. Then he said, "I'm going to tell you something nobody else knows: the reason I'm so good and Troy's so mean. I guess it's about time you understood about your granddaddy. It'll be our secret." I stopped crying. Uncle Charlie began, "You know, times were hard when we were comin' up. There were seven of us kids, and our mother was sick a lot of the time. So before our father died, he lined up all of his children: your great-uncles Jim, John, and Earl; your great-aunts Lillie, Essie, and Della; and your granddaddy and me.

"Your great-granddaddy, George Benjamin, was a really mean man and a poor one to boot. That day, he lined us all up to leave us what he had: a big dose of meanness. I was the baby, and kept running in and out of line as my daddy gave each of his children their dose.

"Somehow as he was givin' it out, he got mixed up 'cause I was runnin' around so, and your granddaddy got *my* dose of meanness, too. So you see, we gotta be extra kind to him. He's had more to bear than the rest of us 'cause all his life he's had to carry around two doses of meanness."

WISDOM FROM THE SWING

A T HIS HOME in Taylorville, Alabama, my grandfather had a swing beneath two giant pecan trees. As he got older, he sat out there and held court. Relatives and friends would come by in the late afternoon, and he would give them his advice on all subjects, whether it was requested or not. He would tell them of the stock market crash of '29 when he lost his Model T Ford, and how you never bought what you couldn't pay for.

He would say never be beholden, be your own person, owe no man. As I sit here owing my soul to Mastercard, I wish I had profited more from his wisdom.

Granddaddy always attended funerals, but never weddings. At a funeral, he would say, the person's troubles were over, but at a wedding they were just beginning. When he didn't attend my wedding, I was terribly hurt; but I remembered his words all too well when I became a single parent, raising three children.

When my grandfather spoke there was no changing his mind. On the rare occasions he wasn't sure of something, he would say he'd have to study on it. He was untrusting of things he didn't understand. I remember walking with him up and down eight flights of stairs as a little child to visit my great-grandmother in the hospital. He was still studying on elevators. I wish I had studied a lot harder on many of my decisions.

If someone was leaving town he would simply say, "When you move, you lose." And again, he was right. All the moves I've made caused me to realize you leave a little part of yourself every time you move. You leave old friends and new, possessions not needed—and the expense, even though we thought it justified at the time, is still a loss. But most important, you lose a sense of belonging and of being a real part of the community. After so many moves, you eventually lose touch with your family and even a closeness within yourself.

There were times, I admit, when I thought Granddaddy a little eccentric, but I realized he was from another place in time. He said anything north of Highway 59 was too far north, full of alley bats, gypsies, and Yankees — Highway 59 was less than ten miles from our house. He felt a great sense of security knowing the people in the community and their families all seemed to share the same values. Strangers could eventually be accepted, but they had to prove themselves first. Granddaddy said a man who would lie would steal, and a man who would lie and steal was capable of anything.

Now about Yankees—he never forgave them. Pa Lucas had told him too many horror stories about the battles of his regiment, the proud Forty-fourth Alabama Infantry, and about his capture and incarceration at Elmira Prison in New York.

My grandfather believed it was very important to know as much about your roots as possible. He said if you don't know where you came from, it's hard to know where you're going. The relatives were used for role models. Stories of their overcoming obstacles and hardships were told to us so we could learn how to cope, drawing from the wisdom of our ancestors. He kept the family Bible on the table near his chair, and he could read well enough to look up a relative that might lend us some guidance.

My grandfather and grandmother never fought. I sincerely believe that this was partly because of my grandmother's near saintly demeanor, but also because Granddaddy thought fighting and arguing did not bring constructive solutions. If a couple was arguing, Granddaddy would say they were not geein' and hawin'. When you plow a mule, he goes left when you say gee and right when you say haw, and you have nice, neat rows. But if the mule doesn't gee and haw, you end up with quite a crooked mess.

My grandfather never turned away a hungry person from our back door — and many came — but there were rules and they would not be broken. No one drank alcohol of any kind on his property and never to his knowledge in front of his wife, children, or grandchildren. It was a well-known rule. One afternoon, though, our maid's husband got drunk and stopped by to see her. My grandfather had cautioned Charlie before, but in this condition his memory had escaped him. Granddaddy had to be about seventy at the time, but he picked up Charlie, threw him into the back of his pickup truck and drove him home, dumping him out in his own yard. Charlie sustained a broken leg during the ordeal. He came back after that on crutches, but never returned in any condition other than stone sober.

Once when we were at the barn milking the cows, a cow kicked him. Granddaddy kicked her back and finished the milking with a broken toe. Needless to say, I *never* had to get a spanking from my grandfather. He could call me sternly by both my given names, and whatever I was doing came to a screeching halt.

He didn't like my playing upstairs in the big old house because the stairs were terribly steep and my Aunt Lou had taken a fall. But I would sneak up there to "meddle," as he called it. Once, after he found me out, he pulled me up into his big lap and pointed to the twenty-foot ceiling.

"You see the brown outline on the ceiling?" he said.

"Yes, sir."

"See the shape of the man? He's dead up there and his blood seeps through."

No matter how many times they painted that ceiling, the brown outline would mysteriously reappear. It was many years later that I ventured back upstairs, and only after learning that an overturned honey bucket had created the outline. In the summer, when it would get hot, the brown line always reappeared.

My grandfather would not tolerate bad language or disrespect in *any* fashion. Once my five-year-old son, Courtney, climbed to the top of one of his big pecan trees. Granddaddy told him to come down immediately, but my son continued to enjoy the view from his lofty perch. Granddaddy fired once over his head with a double-barreled shotgun. Courtney was quickly out of the tree and at my side.

"Mother! Mother! Granddaddy tried to shoot me!"

"Well, then, maybe you better mind him," I said.

My grandfather was a big man, over six feet tall and two hundred and seventy pounds. I always thought of him like John Wayne or Bear Bryant. He was one thing in my life that was always constant, and I felt safe as I walked at his side holding his giant hand.

We buried him April 23, 1987, at the age of eighty-nine, next to my mother and my Uncle Rip. Six of the Fikes grandchildren stood as pallbearers. He was a link to our past and was respected by more than he knew. As I drove up to the old house after the funeral, I looked at the swing between the two pecan trees and realized I would never again see him there. Then I began remembering the words that he had left to guide us.

They called him the Mayor of Taylorville, but I just called him Papa Troy.

Papa Troy

MY 1ST CAMPAIGN

*I*N 1958 I was in the seventh grade at St. John's Elementary. Every afternoon I had to wait from the time I got out of school at 3:00 until my dad got off work at the Alabama Power Company at 5:00 to catch a ride home. During those two hours, I meandered through downtown Tuscaloosa going to the candy store if I had money for black licorice, stopping off at the grave of a dog named "One" that was buried by the Hayes Ambulance driveway, walking past the Ritz theater and checking out the marquee, or just looking in the store windows.

One afternoon as I sauntered through downtown, I noticed the front of the old Burkhalter Hotel was covered with a big sign that read, "George C. Wallace for Governor." I went in and a man gave me a button to put on my shirt. That night when I got home, Mother asked where I got the button. She explained that I had been in Mr. Wallace's campaign headquarters and all the people there were working to help him get elected. Mother said she and Aunt Lou had gone to County High School with Mr. Wallace's wife, Lurleen Burns.

Anyway, I don't know that I planned to go back the next day; knowing me, I probably didn't. But the next afternoon I found myself in front of the Burkhalter again. I went in and asked the man behind the counter if there was something I could do to help Mr. Wallace beat Mr. Patterson. "Well, certainly, little lady. How's about you taking these bumper stickers outside and see how many people you can get to put them on their cars."

"Sure," I said. Every day after that I went to the campaign headquarters. Sometimes I gave out leaflets or pins, but mostly bumper stickers. I handed them to a lot of people saying, "I hope you'll vote for George Wallace for governor."

Cars left unattended during the campaign did not leave Tuscaloosa without a bumper sticker. Usually I put them on the back and the front bumpers so they could be seen coming or going. Sometimes I'd get carried away and put them on telephone poles and store windows. Every bumper sticker they gave me got plastered somewhere.

One Monday afternoon I went in as usual to get my stickers, and the man behind the counter said we wouldn't be giving things away anymore because Tuesday was election day. As I turned to go he said, "Wait. Mr. Wallace wants to see you." My first thought was to run. I thought I'd probably done something wrong, but the man behind the desk said, "Follow me." Reluctantly, I followed him upstairs and down a long dark hall. I felt just like I was being taken to the principal's office.

He stopped, then opened a door. "Here's the little girl you asked for," he told the dark-haired man smoking a cigar. The man motioned for me to come in. Then he removed the cigar from his mouth and spoke, "What's your name young lady?"

"Mary Jean Fielder," I replied softly.

He leaned toward me and smiled. "I wanted to meet you so I could thank you personally for helping us out every afternoon."

"You're welcome," I said perking up. "It was no big deal, I had to wait on my daddy anyway." That didn't sound right, so I quickly added, "but I really do want you to be governor."

"Why?" he grinned at me.

"Well . . ." I started slowly and picked up speed. "Granddaddy says you don't like outsiders or the federal government telling us what to do, and anyway it's against the Constitution. Granddaddy and Grandmother are going to vote for you. Besides, Mother and Aunt Lou said you had to be a good man to be married to Miss Lurleen." I took a breath. He laughed. It didn't hurt my feelings, though; it wasn't a mean laugh. It was a happy laugh. He stood up and shook my hand.

"It was a pleasure to meet you, Miss Mary Jean Fielder." Since he had my hand and called me Miss, a curtsy seemed called for. I turned and skipped down the hallway. He had made me feel like I had done something right for a change. I felt very special.

In 1958, George Wallace lost his first bid for governor of the state of Alabama to John Patterson . . . and I cried.

UNDERNEATH THE OLD OAK TREES

THAT FIRST DAY at Tuscaloosa High School, I was quite a piece of work. I was barely five feet tall, weighed seventy-eight pounds, was flat-chested, big-lipped and had a horrible Toni Perm Mother had given me. I looked like an old Halo shampoo commercial. My clothes weren't exactly fashionable, and I looked like country mouse come to town.

I was scared but also excited and very curious. At St. John's I graduated with a group of seven other students, yet here I was with over three hundred just in my class. There I had been forced to learn and study by Sister Barbara, but here I just had to be at the right place at the right time before class started. I didn't know it then, but I was slightly dyslexic. This meant I knew the difference between up and down, but right and left and the east and west wings were just a puzzling maze. I had to carry all my books because I would get lost going to my locker and be tardy to class.

I guess most teenagers wonder why they are in high school. I know I did. The one thing I knew for sure was, after kissing Bob Tabaca in the closet at St. John's, I didn't want to be a nun.

The other kids at Tuscaloosa High on that first day seemed to know what to do, who to speak to, and what group they were a part of. I had never been a part of a group. I found out that if you spoke to the wrong crowd, they looked at you funny, like who are you to speak to me. I didn't know cheerleaders, football players, and popular kids didn't speak to the people who studied hard (the bookworms) or the leftovers (the misfits, oddballs and nerds).

You could identify the unpopular kids because they wore glasses, or their pants were pulled up too high, their clothes didn't match or didn't fit. Some of them looked poor. I didn't know if I was poor or not, but I knew I wasn't rich. They gave us I.Q. tests so we would know if we were smart or not. They told me my I.Q. was 110. Someone else said that below 90 you were a moron, so at least that settled one thing. I knew I didn't belong with the smart people. It also helped me choose my subjects. I took general math instead of algebra and choral music because I liked to sing.

My freshman year, I guess you would say I kept a pretty low profile and studied on things, the other kids and their groups. Before the school year was over, I had straightened out my perm and pulled my hair back in a ponytail. I starched and ironed white shirts and wore them with some straight skirts Mother had gotten me from a friend. I had nice legs, but the skirts were so long nobody knew it. My adolescence was so delayed I skipped acne, but my lips were still big. I used to put lipstick just on the center of the inside trying to make them look smaller.

I finally decided I wanted to be in the popular crowd. They seemed to be so much wiser, and they laughed easier and louder. They teased each other and cut up more. I figured the only way to be immediately accepted was to be a cheerleader, so the entire month of April I stayed after school practicing my cheers and twisting my limbs. That part really wasn't so hard. I was limber; I could jump, do splits, backbends, walk on my hands and do flips, and it was fun. I decided I was really going to like being a cheerleader. Most of the people who were practicing with me were in the in-crowd. They thought I was funny, and at least they remembered my name and spoke to me.

Who's got a team . . . who's got a yell. We got a team that fights like Helen in a high chair . . . Who put her up there Maw . . . Paw . . . sis-boom-bah!!

Grandmother would not have liked that cheer. She used to say even when you said darn you thought the other and, well, Helen made you think it even though we didn't actually say it. Anyway, I really had to work on screaming. I had been taught to be quiet at St. John's for six years. I spoke very softly, and yelling took some work. They broke us up into teams of three, and we would cheer together. I was really getting excited . . . this is what I wanted to be. Popular or not, I wanted to wear those skirts, twirl around, yell and show my legs.

The weekend before tryouts I went on a picnic and ended up with poison ivy all over me. The worse part was . . . yep, on my legs. They were red and raw by Sunday. I was sitting on the front porch crying and scratching. My dad came out on the porch and saw me. He hadn't seen me cry very often. I told him I had cheerleader tryouts and my legs looked awful.

Dad had one of his well-meaning brainstorms. He said, "You know, some guys in the army got poison ivy. The medics put tannic acid on them, and it went away in no time." My dad was going to save the day. Tomorrow, on his way back from work he would stop by the drugstore. This was great! He was going to pour it on my legs Monday night. I'd have Tuesday to heal, then cheerleader tryouts on Wednesday. Everything would be fine.

Monday afternoon I ran out to meet Dad. He had remembered. I put on a pair of shorts and we went out on the porch. He doused both my legs front and back. I thought it might sting a little, but all of a sudden I felt like a human french fry.

Well, I never knew how the mix-up occurred, but somehow he had purchased a bottle of carbolic acid.

I ran into the house to get into the bathtub. My little brother hadn't locked the door. He was sitting in a tub full of water screaming for me to get out of the bathroom. I was screaming at him to get out of the bathtub. Mother came in behind Dad trying to find out what the dickens was going on.

My dad took me to the hospital. We didn't say a word all the way. I knew he felt terrible. I will never forget it. He sat down under a "No Smoking — Oxygen In Use" sign, smoking a

Chesterfield, then he spoke. "Don't worry about it, hon . . . I'm going to buy you some really pretty long pants," and he patted my arm. That was my dad and that was the end of my being a cheerleader.

The next day I went to school on crutches with yellow furrison ointment oozing from gauze bandages. I went to cheerleader tryouts and waited as the other girls went in. I didn't cry, but I wanted to. After the blisters healed, I had bright pink scars I carried throughout high school. I never thought about going out for cheerleader again.

THERE WERE SO many distractions in high school for me. It was not a place to study, and I began dating. My first date was a big mistake. A boy named Tommy Davis had a nice smile and he and his girlfriend, Anna, had broken up. So I decided to ask him to the CYO Dance (Catholic Youth Organization). I couldn't believe it when I finally got up the nerve to ask him and he said, "yes," right away. I didn't know that he wanted Anna to be jealous, or that she would be! She caught me in the hall after the dance. I felt awful. I wanted to tell her that she did not have to worry about Tommy going out with me ever again, but I wasn't sure what to tell her.

Tommy had taken me to the CYO and we danced to a few songs, drank some punch, met Sister Barbara and Father Buerio, then he said he was bored and wanted to leave. It was early, and

I didn't want to go, but we went to Art's Charhouse and had french fries and a Coke. Then he drove straight to a turn that said University Place School. He knew exactly where he was going.

It was dark behind the school, and he drove up to the curb and parked the car. The radio was on. He slid one arm on the back of the seat and put his other arm around me. Then he pulled me toward him pressing his lips against mine. I froze . . . tears suddenly began squirting from my eyes. I couldn't speak. I know he was actually a nice boy because he kept saying, "I'm sorry, I'm sorry, I'm sorry, please don't cry. I am taking you home right now, I promise."

He and Anna got back together. From then on when Tommy would see me in the hall, he would smile and I could feel my face flush. After a while Anna forgave me, and she became one of my first friends from the in-crowd.

I WAS AN unmitigated disaster as a date. They should have taught dating 101 in high school. I would put on four or five pairs of underpants, two or three whole slips and then wear a wide, tight belt so I would look at least like I had hips. There was no way a guy could cop a feel from me as neither one of us would have felt anything through all that underwear.

Soon after the fiasco with Tommy Davis came a date with Donny Hinton. We went to a party at the Thomases' cabin. Before that night I never had seen kids drink, and I never had seen anyone drunk except Uncle Rip. When we got in the car to leave, Donny came toward me. I thought I could handle a kiss, but this boy stuck his tongue in my mouth, so I did what came natural . . . I bit the blood out of him. He screamed at me, told me I was crazy, and took me home.

What was even worse, Monday at school everybody had heard about it. Estest Hayes, whom I later realized was the self-elected morals guardian for our class, gave me a lecture on how I was getting a terrible reputation for kissing boys on the first date. Then I was really confused, but relieved. At least now I knew what the rules were: you don't let boys kiss you until the third date and you keep your lips pressed tight so they can't get their tongues in. Boy, I was glad to have that straightened out.

I started sitting in front of the mirror practicing what I would say on a date so I could be cool. But cool wasn't what I was. At first I must have been funny, then just plain hilarious. Mother was worried about me. She asked why the boys only asked me out once and never called again. I certainly couldn't tell her it was because I already had such a horrible reputation or that I had really changed and didn't kiss boys on the first date anymore.

Things got a little better by the eleventh grade, but everything was still so confusing. A few guys even lasted until the third date and received my kiss, but boy did that bring on a new set of problems. Sister Barbara had warned us about impure thoughts, but, I'm here to tell you, at old THS those thoughts ran rampant.

Finally, during my junior year, I experienced what I thought love was . . . a boy, a girl, and Johnny Mathis. The boy's name was Ray Thomas. He gave me his ring and asked me to go steady. Now I had an identity, Ray's girlfriend. I was part of a couple. When he asked me to go steady I said yes; but he never said *he* would, and the ring, well . . . his dad owned a jewelry store. My first broken heart. I couldn't listen to Johnny Mathis for a long time. Both of them had disappointed me terribly.

I was learning now, but what I wanted more than just to learn was to understand, and understanding continued to elude me. I had earned my place on the fringe of the popular crowd. I wore Moxie Loafers with white bobbysocks and, yes, I had a gray poodle skirt with a pink poodle on it.

Then I met the boy with whom I would spend the next twenty-two years of my life. I saw him at a dance at the Fort Brandon Armory doing some risqué moves he called the Mississippi Roll. Big shoulders and killer green eyes. He was a year younger and seemed so much easier to talk to. His favorite song was "He's So Vain" and mine was "He's So Fine" and Diana Ross was singing "Stop in the Name of Love." I didn't listen to Diana Ross or my mother. It's funny how this thing called love hides the obvious.

The night after my senior prom my mom was in a serious car accident that left her in a coma for ten years. I only went back to school one day after that to take my final exams. I couldn't go back because I was afraid to leave Mother, and I didn't like people feeling sorry for me. I'd always thought bad things were headlines in the newspapers that happened to other people.

Although I managed to take my exams and pass, from 1959 to 1963 I don't think I had learned very much more than I already knew scholastically. Yet I had learned a lot more about life. Now that the dust has settled, I realize those are the lessons I've taken with me.

Recently, I returned to my thirtieth class reunion. As we stood singing the "Alma Mater" it was so strange. When I stood up, I saw myself in the old gym in a 28-AAA bra, skinny, big-lipped and overpermed. Only now I was with friends I had known for almost three decades. I no longer felt I had to fit in a group or dress like anybody else. Anna was standing next to me. I turned and smiled at her. My four years in high school seemed like they were only yesterday.

> Underneath the old oak trees where the breezes sigh,
> Loveliest of our memories
> Tuscaloosa High
> T.H.S. — T.H.S. We are all for you
> We will ever sing thy praise
> To you will ere be true

A DIME FOR DADDY

T HE AFTERNOON before my first big date, my dad called me outside. "I want you to watch me change this tire," he said as he jacked up the right rear of our '56 Plymouth. I quietly took a seat on the edge of the porch, unquestioning for fear that he might change his mind and not let me go.

"Now, you change it," he said. As I finished popping the hubcap back in place he looked at his watch. "Now, do it again." My dad was serious about this tire business. Quietly, I began again. This time when I replaced the hubcap, he said, "Time: fifteen minutes." He looked at me sternly saying, "If you're ever over fifteen minutes late, don't tell me you had a flat tire."

"Yes, sir." I said.

My dad was obviously having a really difficult time with my impending womanhood. It was not only obvious to me, but to anyone within four miles. We lived on top of a big hill, and the three new dusk-to-dawn lights Dad had installed could be seen from as far away as the viaduct on Greensboro Road.

The huge lights made our yard look like a football field from off in the distance. He had one over each end of the house and the third over the driveway. When my date and I would pull up into the drive, my dad's face would appear in the dining room window. As we reached the porch, the front door would fly open, and Dad would push on the screen saying, "Good night, son," dismissing my date. Then he'd close the door in his face, with me safely on the inside.

I couldn't understand, for the life of me, why my dating had caused my dad to act so peculiar. He tried to assure me that he trusted *me*, but it was obvious he didn't trust any of my dates.

When my dates came to pick me up, Dad looked at each one of them when he shook their hands as if he wanted to crawl through their eyeballs and see what they were thinking. Then, as we would turn to leave, he'd hand me a dime for the phone and tell me to put it in my shoe. While I placed the dime, he would stare at my date saying to me that if there was any sort of trouble just to call him, and he'd be right there. Until I was seventeen, he never let me leave the house without a dime in my shoe.

A few days after the tire changing episode, Dad apparently felt compelled to have a father-daughter sex talk with me. He began muttering about all boys wanting the same thing, that I should sit way over on my side of the car, always keep my legs crossed, and *never* wear dark eye makeup or red lipstick. We were in the car at the time, and I remember being so embarrassed that I briefly contemplated jumping from the moving vehicle.

The day that I got married, he was really weird. He was more nervous than I was. As we started down the aisle, I was fine until he began asking me questions: if I was OK, if I was afraid, if I was sure I was doing the right thing. As I held onto his arm, I couldn't tell which of us was shaking worse, but my dress suddenly weighed so much I could barely drag it down the aisle. It was inconceivable that he would wait until that moment to ask if I had doubts, but then my dad wasn't like other people.

After the ceremony, he seemed calmer than he had been since I was fourteen years old. I guess he felt like I was no longer his responsibility, and he seemed greatly relieved. My dad had been raised in a Catholic orphanage by the Sisters of Charity; he had no idea how a real family interacted. He became a man, a husband, and a father, with only a vague idea of how he was supposed to behave. And he made a lot of mistakes. When I got older, I realized he did his best. Dad died May 17, 1992, exactly twenty years to the day after my mother. The last thing he did for me was install a new dusk-to-dawn light over my driveway. As I stand at the kitchen window watching my fifteen-year-old daughter and her date disappear into the darkness beyond Dad's light, I believe I understand him so much better now.

Dad, I think I did a better job than you did with the sex talk. I made sure she had a quarter for the telephone, but I'm still scared. I can't help but wonder would she be safer or would I feel any better if, this afternoon, I had taught her how to change a tire.

EVERYTHING IN ITS OWN TIME

IN MAY 1963 while turning into our driveway, my mother was hit broadside by an oncoming car. As a result of her injuries, she spent the last ten years of her life in a coma. During that time, no matter where she was . . . at home, in the hospital, or the nursing home, my grandmother was with her. Even though there was nothing medically that could be done, Grandmother stayed, bathed her, rubbed her with lotion, and always she talked to her.

Grandmother said she knew Mother was there and could hear her. I was not so sure, but because Grandmother believed it, I talked to her, too. After a couple of years, the hope that Mother would eventually wake up began to fade, but never entirely.

She suffered terrible infections of all kinds . . . pneumonia, constant kidney and bladder infections, bed sores, and seizures. She was fed through a tube and was catheterized. It was heartbreaking to watch a beautiful thirty-eight-year-old woman who loved to dance and had such a great smile just wither away.

When she died on May 17, 1972, Grandmother was still

with her. Mother's auburn hair was steel gray, and her atrophied little body weighed only seventy pounds.

WHEN MOM'S ACCIDENT occurred, it was the morning after my junior/senior prom. I was seventeen. At first all I did was pray and beg God, no matter what condition she was in, to please not take her. I was hopeful, even though the doctors said it was a miracle she was alive with the amount of brain damage she had incurred. I still believed one day Mom would wake up. For years I would sit by her bed listening to her breathe, waiting for her eyes to open and know me.

Mother missed my high school graduation, my wedding, and the birth of my two sons. Eventually, my little brother and sister were no longer children. By then I began to think that maybe she would be sad if she woke up and realized how much of our lives she had missed. But the next day I would say she had looked so forward to being a grandmother and would be thrilled about her two grandsons, and somehow she would adjust.

Her appearance changed drastically. We knew she was partially blind and would never use her left arm or leg. Her nose had become stretched and misshapen from the levine tube. She used to laugh and say that when she was a little girl she would put a clothespin on her nose so when she grew up it would look regal.

Finally, I no longer wanted her to wake up. It would all have been too overwhelming. She wasn't even allowed to age gracefully. She was only forty-eight, but she looked so old and pitiful.

She was sick all the time now, and I began asking God to please take her. I felt so guilty and selfish for my earlier prayer, but sometimes I felt guilty for asking Him to let it end.

There were times I felt guilty praying for her to die, and I would question myself. Was I asking so she wouldn't have to hurt anymore, was I asking for myself, for Grandmother, or the rest of the family? Ten years was a long time. As a family during those years, we learned a lot about ourselves and each other. At different times for our own reasons, I'm sure we all wished she had died in the accident; but I believe I can honestly say that none of us ever thought about helping her die.

I know for a fact that neither my grandmother nor I could have ever considered removing Mother's levine tube to watch her slowly starve to death. I never heard anyone in our family say anything remotely like that. If they thought it, they never said it aloud. Not that I thought that we were better than others . . . just that in our hearts we knew it was wrong.

My grandmother, a soft-spoken, chubby little woman, not quite five feet tall, who never cursed and never demanded, set an example for us all through both her words and her actions. She showed us what true love was . . . caring, unselfish and compassionate; what we as a family and as human beings were to do, even to one of His most pitiful brethren.

Grandmother was an example not only for us but for anyone

who had the good fortune to know her. She knew right from wrong, black from white, and good from evil. There were no special "extenuating" circumstances. What was right was always right, and what was wrong was wrong. She was steadfast, and I will be eternally grateful for her strength.

After Mother died, I didn't know how to plan the funeral because she had converted to Catholicism. Except for her immediate family, Mother's other relatives were Baptist, and we all thought of their minister, Brother Tatum, as a member of the family. I asked Grandmother what Dad and I should do about the funeral, and she said, "You do what your mother would have wanted you to."

Well, I knew what she half-jokingly said to me once. "Funerals are a ridiculous expense. Just stick me in a pine box and dump me in a ditch somewhere. Then tell all my friends not to spend their hard-earned money on flowers that are just going to be left in the sun to die."

Mother had only a floral casket blanket. In lieu of flowers, we had her friends donate money to charity and the nursing home in her name. I think this is what she would have wanted.

At the service, I asked the organist to play "Amazing Grace" and "The Old Rugged Cross" after Mother's favorite song, "The Ave Maria," hoping they would make our Baptist family members feel more comfortable. None of them had ever been inside a Catholic church before. As mass began, the priest came out in the seasonal robe. Then the altar boy draped the black robe for the mass of the dead around his shoulders. At the benediction they draped him with a white robe.

My Great-uncle Jim and my Great-aunt Evie were sitting toward the back of the church. As the altar boy draped the white robe on the priest, my sweet, hard-of-hearing, *very* deep-voiced Aunt Evie whispered to my Uncle Jim, "One thing about these Catholics, we sure don't have to worry about them freezing to death. They've got plenty of coats."

My dad, brother, sister and I were up in the second pew with Grandmother. We heard Aunt Evie along with everybody else in the church. She had provided comic relief where it is not usually found. I couldn't help it. I covered my mouth to stifle my laughter. Grandmother cut her eyes at me as if to say, "How can you possibly be laughing at your own mother's funeral?". I leaned over and touched her arm. "It's all right, Mother's laughing too," I said, trying not to giggle. For the first time in a very long while, my grandmother smiled.

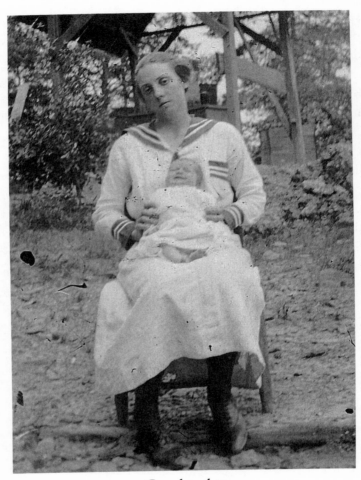

Grandmother

HER GIFT

FROM MY earliest childhood recollections, strangers brought newborns to my grandmother's back door. She would take them in her arms, cover their small mouths with hers and blow into them three times. The strangers would then thank her and retrieve their infants, leaving fresh eggs, vegetables, or some sign of their coming.

Years went by before I even questioned why they came. Grandmother said blowing in the babies' mouths was supposed to prevent the thrush or thrash. I was still puzzled as to why they brought the babies to my grandmother. Later she explained that if your father dies before you are born, it is said that you receive a special gift because of your loss.

William Avery Lewis, Grandmother's father, died of typhoid fever three months before she was born. The baby was to have been named after him had it been a boy. Subsequently, she was named Willie Avery Lewis, a name which she hated yet carried with pride.

She told me even as a small child she was sent for and carried by wagon to the bedside of the sick. I thought it must have been frightening for a small child to be so often in the presence of illness, dying and death. From her I never heard anything but acceptance and a willingness to go.

After she was married, she still went to stay and help with family members who were ill or having babies. My grandfather never liked Grandmother to leave his side, but seemed to expect and want her to go when she was called on these occasions. It was as if he felt it was her duty.

When my first son was born, I brought him to Grandmother and placed him in her arms. "Will you blow in Lance's mouth?" I asked. She grinned up at me and asked if I believed the old wives' tale. "I don't know," I said," but if you do have the gift, I think you should share it with your great-grandson."

Grandmother blew in all my children's mouths, rolled their livers, shaped their heads and gave them foul-smelling remedies for their illnesses. I'm still not sure I believed she could prevent disease, but I do know that her mere presence brought a sense of peace in crisis, comfort in pain, and her touch was the sincerest form of love and affection I have ever known.

THREE WORDS FOR MOMMY

A S MY HUSBAND left for work, I asked him to please try to get home early so we could take Lance trick-or-treating. He stopped and turned toward me. "Do what?" he said.

I persisted, almost pleading, "I've already got him a costume, a kitten outfit."

"That is absurd. He's barely eighteen months old! Furthermore, he can't even *say* 'trick or treat.'" Subject and door closed.

Well, I began to discuss the subject further with *myself* as I heard the car crank. The objection is Lance can't say "trick or treat," so I'll teach him, the objection is now overcome.

I put Lance up on the kitchen table and sat in a chair in front of him with a large bag of M & M's. "Listen to Mommy, Lance. You and I are going to have lots of fun tonight, but first you have to learn to say some magic words." After a while and several M & M's, he tired of the game and went down for his nap. After lunch I began again. "Watch Mommy's mouth — they're funny words: trick-or-treat, trick-or-treat. Watch Mommy." Finally he blurted out, "twick-a-tweat," like Bambi trying to say bird. We marched all through the house singing *twick-a-tweat*. When his dad came home, Lance was all dressed up in his kitty-cat suit. His father took one look at him, then at me, and said, "I told you already, he's not going; he can't even say 'trick or treat.'"

"Twick-a-tweat!" Lance popped up like Pavlov's dog waiting for an M & M, and his father rolled his eyes in defeat.

Children give adults an opportunity to enjoy things of their childhood again, only this time through the child's eyes. We got to the first house, and I showed Lance where the doorbell was. I told him when they answered the door, he had to say the magic words.

A nice lady holding a large, overflowing basket of candy looked at Lance for a moment then bent down to him and smiled. "What do you say?" she asked. And he said it — "Twick a tweat!"

She laughed and put two huge handfulls of candy in the pumpkin sack I had given him. He saw other children running to the next house, so he tore out as fast as his short little legs would carry him and ran up to the door. The lady had seen him coming and waited. He held open his pumpkin sack. He was so excited. He looked up at her, then glanced in my direction for help, but before I could remind him, he yelled out, "Candy!"

The woman began to laugh, and I whispered the magic words. He repeated them and watched as the lady put more treats in the pumpkin bag. His eyes were so big and such a beautiful green. He would look up at the nice people who opened the doors and then look in his sack as if he were seeing a miracle. He didn't stop long enough to eat any of the candy; he was a tiny man on a mission. Or maybe the poor thing was still full of M & M's.

I followed him up to the end of the street until the little legs stopped running and began walking slower and slower. I picked him up as he held on tightly to his pumpkin sack. His sleepy head rested on my shoulder. The air smelled so clean, and the sky was just full of stars as I walked along carrying my precious kitty-cat past the other goblins.

He's twenty-five now, and he's grown quite tired of this story. But every Halloween I remember the little kitty-cat that said, "twick-a-tweat."

Granddaddy and Grandmother

THE BIGGEST PORK CHOP

O NE NIGHT as my son and I sat down to supper, he said, "No butter on my bread, Mom."

I gave him a puzzled look. His father never ate butter, but he always had. "I can't eat butter. Dad's out of town, so I'm the man of the house."

Lance was only three years old at the time, but since that evening twenty-one years ago he's never eaten butter. This may seem insignificant, but it made me think about our parents as role models and how we identify with our same-sex parent.

My role model, I realized, was my grandmother who lived next door. I ate everything she did (with the exception of pickled peaches). I would sit with her during Christmas, and we would share entire boxes of chocolate-covered cherries.

As I look back, I believe I patterned my role as a wife and mother after her. No wonder I get so confused—I'm a generation behind my peers.

She used to lay out my grandfather's clothes, even his towel and bath cloth, and she always served him first at mealtime. I can remember waiting impatiently as she sorted through mounds of fried chicken or pork chops to select the biggest one for him. Then she would set my grandfather's plate at the head of the table.

In these small ways, she seemed to reaffirm him as head of the household and show him he was special. Grandfather, on the other hand, never let her work in the garden, and he prided himself on carrying things he told her were too heavy. He even hired a lady to help her with housework. Although I remember her asking for very little, Grandfather never denied her anything.

If my grandfather was ill, Grandmother treated him like a child with a terminal illness. And when my grandmother got sick, he did everything he knew how to reciprocate her kindness. There was a fairness to it all.

When I was about twelve, I was at their house when Grandmother came home from the hospital after surgery. She came in the door by the living room and sat in a chair. My grandfather knelt down, took her hands and kissed them saying, "I love you." I had never seen affection shared between them, but I will never forget the way she looked at him.

When my grandfather died, their marriage had spanned sixty-seven years, and the roles they had chosen in this union seemed to have suited them.

Now Grandmother's gone, too, and so many changes have taken place — changes that make it much more difficult to clearly identify roles.

With the advent of equal rights, working moms, abortion, sexual discrimination suits, single parents, divorce, and the feminist movement, I find myself in quite a quandary.

I guess it's no wonder it takes me forever just to serve supper because I can't decide who should get the biggest pork chop.

NORTH OF THE MASON-DIXON LINE

*I*N 1977 MY first husband worked for a real estate development company in Pensacola, Florida, and he was offered quite a promotion. The only negative seemed to be that we would have to move to the home office in Troy, Michigan, a suburb outside of Detroit. He made this timely announcement as I walked in from the hospital with our third child, a three-day-old baby girl. Happy and excited over his new opportunity, he began his campaign to assure me and the children that we would love the North.

My mind began to imagine what it would be like in our golden years, sitting in rocking chairs on the nursing home porch, hearing him say something like, "You know, hon, my *only* regret in life is I'll always wonder just what our lives would have been like if *you'd* gone to Detroit with me back in '77."

I began to feel guilty for not letting him know how proud I was of him and for my less than enthusiastic congratulations. But I didn't need him to make me feel guilty; over the years I had become the travel agent for guilt trips. Finally we reached a compromise — Detroit would simply be an "interim situation." It would look impressive on his resume. Now what kind of wife would I be not to give one measly year of my life to further my husband's career.

I was born in Tuscaloosa, Alabama, and the furthest north I had ever lived was Birmingham. As my mood and personality began to change, I knew they would say I simply had postpartum depression. But it had nothing to do with my hormones.

I was having nightmares and the dream was always the same. There was a giant map of the United States with a big red line separating the North and South. In my dream I was a donkey sitting on my haunches on the Southern side of the Mason-Dixon with my bottom covering northern Alabama and Tennessee.

My husband stood angrily on the Northern side of the red line with a large rope knotted like a hangman's noose around my neck, cursing and screaming obscenities as he tried to drag me across the imaginary line. I remained steadfast with my front legs stretched straight out to prevent the horror I was sure lay ahead.

I always woke about the time that my breath was totally cut off and my body about to be dragged onto Northern soil. It didn't take a Ph.D. in psychology to interpret my dream. I've heard it said dreams are often prophetic. . . .

MY HUSBAND went ahead of us leaving me as usual with the packing and the children. I had grown accustomed to it, but this time it was much more difficult, especially with the new baby. The boys were older and had formed some very special friendships.

They had to give away the mighty Isis, our cock-a-poo, and dispose of three aquariums of named fish they tearfully doled out to their buddies.

As we pulled out of the driveway, waving to our neighbors, I turned and took one long last look at our two-story, white columned, antebellum home with its majestic old oaks and the two magnolias I had planted in the front yard.

Our younger son, Courtney, was still crying when we crossed the Illinois state line. The only time he had stopped crying was while we ate our last meal at the northernmost location of Morrison's Cafeteria in Kentucky. It was obvious we were leaving everything familiar; even little things were different: red-topped clover in Illinois is lavender.

The price of houses in the frozen tundra was staggering, quality construction a myth, grade-A wood a joke. We were forced to buy a house in a subdivision, where there were *no* trees, in the middle of a field.

The house was not ready yet, so for three-and-a-half weeks we existed in a two-room hotel suite with a baby and a five- and a seven-year-old. I had to keep the phone under the bed. The seven-year-old had found something he liked about the North: room service. The boys were creative in finding things to entertain themselves. They raced elevators or they would just press Stop and take their matchbox cars inside to play. Once Courtney followed a balloon onto the ledge of the fifth floor and was removed by the hotel manager from an adjoining balcony.

We finally moved into the house. Now there is the word *complete* and there is the word *finished*. I thought I was nearly finished, but the house was not complete. Our home in Pensacola had hardwood floors, plantation shutters, solid brass light fixtures, wallpaper, dentil molding and a mahogany stairwell. What we had in Michigan, however, was not a home. It was a giant cracker-box surrounded by dirt. It was bitterly cold at times; the arctic wind even ripped through the wall plugs to bite our ankles.

WHERE I WAS raised, we got up when it was daylight and went to bed when it was dark. Up north I had to tell three little children at eight-thirty it was bedtime when it was broad daylight outside. Try explaining Northern lights, then wake them up in pitch black dark and tell them it's time to get up. I'm sure they thought their mother had forgotten to pack her mind.

Did you know that the Midwest has the highest incidence of child abuse in the country, and most all of the houses have basements? Basements are where they keep their pale, hollow-eyed, abused offspring.

My husband assured me that this was an exceptionally cold winter as the windchill off the Great Lakes dipped to minus forty-five degrees. The first time I heard the radio announcer issue the warning to keep small children in their homes, I didn't understand. We hadn't wanted to go outside since the temperature had dropped below sixty anyway. Then my neighbor explained. These warnings are issued because children run and play with their mouths open. Their lungs freeze and they *die*.

Coca-colas I had left in the garage exploded, and glass and ice hung in strange stalactite fashion from the ceiling and walls.

One afternoon my garage door's rubber seal froze solid to the driveway. As I sat in my car mashing my electric garage door opener to no avail, asphyxiating myself and my poor baby, I thought of my sons running and playing happily in front of the school while their little lungs froze.

When we moved to Michigan all I had were open-toed shoes and I didn't even own a coat. Now we owned snowsuits, sweaters, scarves, mittens, hats, earmuffs, heavy socks, coats, mukluks, galoshes, overshoes and moon boots. No wonder Yankees are in such an all-fired hurry and in a bad mood. They get up in the dark then waste half the day putting on and taking off clothes. My sons had been accustomed to running in and out barefoot with a pair of shorts and maybe a T-shirt. My younger son sat and cried at the inconvenience and cumbersomeness of it all.

One morning after I dropped the boys off at the school, I began to notice the rusty, corroded cars rushing past my new station wagon as it tiptoed through the salted snow and sludge. I turned in at the next gas station and decided after filling up my tank to get my car washed.

As the attendant pumped the gas, he noticed my Florida license plates. "What are you doing up here?" he asked. "My husband brought me," I replied. I certainly didn't want him to think it was my idea. "I'd like to get my car washed," I said.

"You want to get your car washed?" he repeated. "Yes," I answered in the affirmative, wondering if my accent was that difficult to comprehend. He smiled and said, "OK, go right ahead." This was a peculiar morning. A stranger had actually smiled at me.

After the car wash I headed home. The baby was getting sleepy, and I knew if she fell asleep in the car I would wake her up when I tried to take off her snowsuit, then she would be cranky for the remainder of the day. I pulled in my driveway and came to a stop outside the garage, deciding it was too cold to chance being trapped in there again.

I lifted the baby from the car seat and began to pull on the inside of the door handle. The handle moved, but the door didn't open. I repeated the process: nothing. Then I restarted the car and started flipping all the door and window switches. The switches worked, but the windows and doors were frozen shut. And I was trapped — *again*. I looked up and down the street but saw no one. The baby began to cry. I pulled into the neighbor's driveway and honked my horn. I waited, honked again, but there was no response. Up and down the street I went, driving into strangers' driveways honking my horn. By now the baby and I were both crying. Finally a woman peered from a downstairs window. So I began making motions like a retarded mime. She opened the front door slightly, and I began my frantic pantomime again. Cautiously she approached the car. The baby's howling by now, and I was blubbering with exaggerated facial and hand motions trying to make her understand my plight.

She turned and scurried into the house. I wondered who you called in situations like this — the fire department, AAA, or maybe she thought I was crazy and was calling the police. Personally, I no longer cared who she called, or where they took us, as long as it was warm. The front door opened. I thought it was the same lady, but it was hard to tell as she had donned the articles of the arctic.

In one gloved hand she had a long extension cord and in the other — a hair dryer. She began blowdrying the outside of my car door. In the last few months I had learned about tire chains and antifreeze but nobody told me the importance of a good hair dryer.

After our ordeal, the baby had barely gotten to sleep before it was time to pick up the boys. I woke the sleeping infant. She didn't cry. She just lay there staring blankly at me as I put her little arms back in her snowsuit. Heading for the car I began to pray, "Holy Spirit, Merciful Jesus, Heavenly Father, if it be thy will deliver this cup from me." I have developed a tendency in times of extreme stress to call out to the entire Deity.

MY HUSBAND eventually began traveling a lot, checking on the company's holdings in Louisiana and Florida. Every time he left on a plane headed south, I both envied and resented him. The skin on the baby's cheeks peeled off. My lips were cracked, and I had sores on the corners of my mouth. The skin on one of the boy's knees even peeled off from the bitter cold. Our hair stood on end from the static electricity.

The addition of a humidifier to our furnace hadn't seemed to help. The children and I were beginning to deteriorate rapidly. We rarely went out. Our bodies were lathered with Vaseline. Our lips were cracked and swollen, we had ceased trying to comb our hair, and we didn't cry anymore. The boys had quit fighting. Nobody laughed. I couldn't; it cracked my scabs. I found a drugstore that delivered antibiotics and antihistamines for sore throats, stuffy noses, and ear infections. They brought us Kleenex and, of course, Vaseline.

In the Detroit *Free Press* one morning there was a contest, "How many minutes of sunshine will there be in the month of February?" I had begun turning all the lights on in the house, wrapping myself in an afghan, sitting by the furnace trying to remember how the warm rays of the sun felt and imagining azure blue skies, my children's laughter, and birds singing. Maybe were no birds up north because there were no trees, or maybe because they sang with their mouths open, their lungs froze, and they all died.

My husband was in Panama City, Florida, for a week. He wouldn't be home Saturday, he was playing golf with some clients. I began to have sinister, evil thoughts, and it was getting more difficult to have a conversation with him. I reminded him that it was March and we had two and a half months left here. He said he was aware that February was followed by March.

The next week he came home, his face tanned and his forehead showing a slight sunburn. The boys had a twenty-four-hour virus, and the little one had a terrible cold. We were still in our robes and slippers.

"Hi," we said, in feeble unison. His disappointment in us was apparent. He began immediately by saying, "You've never given it a chance, you haven't even tried, just look at you."

"No, thank you," I said. "I'd rather not," knowing in my heart there was a shred of truth in what he said. But he had no idea the toll this existence had on us. We were no longer a family. It had become him versus us.

EASTER CAME, but the snow was too deep outside to hide our Easter eggs. I didn't want the children to think that the Easter Bunny had met with the same fate as the birds, so I hid the eggs in the living room and kitchen. By the end of April, they were finally able to remove the garbage from Christmas. It had been repeatedly covered by the snow plows.

In early May, enough sunlight filtered through to give me the strength to mount another campaign to leave. But my husband had no intention of leaving. He had reneged on our agreement. I told him as he left for work that morning that I was selling the house. "Fine," he said, either not hearing me or not thinking I was capable.

I did sell the house that very day, and the children and I were packing when he returned. Where we were going we didn't exactly know, but wherever it was, it wouldn't be here. We had to wait an extra three days for the boys to make up their snow days, thereby extending our stay to 368 days, three more than I had agreed to.

As we crossed the Alabama-Tennessee line, I pulled into a rest stop with my three weary, travel-worn, Northern-ravaged children. The warmth of the sun caressed us like a grandmother. Blue skies contrasted as beautifully as I had remembered against the verdant green of the magnolia trees. We threw off our socks and shoes and ran barefoot through the soft, *red*-topped clover. Once again my children were laughing . . . and birds, birds were singing, unafraid, with their mouths open.

Ashley, Courtney, Lance

'GOD, I GOT THEM HERE'

MOTHER USED to say to me, "You just wait. One day you'll be grown with children of your own. Then you'll understand."

In church one morning we were singing, "Lord, Here I Am," and I started thinking about Sunday mornings when I was a child. They always seemed the same. Mother would wake us up, try to get us fed, dressed, and to keep us from getting dirty while she threw on her clothes, admonishing Daddy all the while to please hurry up.

Mother would be brushing our hair, pulling it up in neat pony tails, and trying somehow at the same time to help my little brother locate a missing shoe. Daddy'd still be shaving, while Mother would run out zipping her dress to switch one, two, or all three of us for fighting. Then she'd make a public announcement, *"All of You Go to the Bathroom."* Upon getting the three of us in the old green '53 Chevy, she would honk the horn for Daddy. He would finally make his way to the car, and we would begin the eight-mile drive to St. John's. On weekdays Dad normally drove a little fast. On Sundays, though, he drove as if he had no particular place to go.

As we cruised down Greensboro Avenue, Daddy would gaze out the window. Mother would fold her hands on her Bible, and the same conversation would occur — every Sunday. Mother would ask Daddy couldn't he please drive a little faster. Then invariably, the one of us who didn't get a window would begin to whine, "I didn't get a window seat last time either."

As soon as we would get into one of the back pews because we were usually late, Mother would kneel down, her head in her hands, and whisper, "God, I got them here; You'll have to do the rest." At the time, I thought this was a strange Sunday morning prayer.

Then, I had three children of my own. Most of the time I took them to church alone. After settling arguments, finding shoes, combing down cow licks, we would make it there. It always seemed that about the time the service started, I would be reminded of my mother's "strange prayer" just as my daughter would loudly announce to the congregation, "Mommy, I have to tee tee."

I would leave the boys in the pew after whispering, "I have to take your sister to the bathroom. Be quiet. And *don't* touch each other!" Returning as inconspicuously as possible, we would sit down. Opening my prayer book seemed to signal my younger son, Courtney, to begin to squirm. "What's the matter?" I'd ask, knowing full well the answer, "I have to go to the bathroom." And I would ask him the dumbest question: "Why didn't you?" There's no reason to ever ask this question of a child; they have no idea why they didn't.

I would get up again. Down the center aisle I'd go, holding his hand. It was always more embarrassing the second time I had to get up, especially if it was one of the boys, because his other little hand always held on to the problem. Sometimes, I would glance to the left or right.

The women my age didn't pay any attention, but the older ones were smiling just like I bet Mother would have been. When I'd finally get back, the boys would start the touching game: touch, touch, shove, pinch, hit. Grabbing one by the arm, I would place myself between them. "But I wanted to sit by you, Mommy!" my daughter would pout. So I'd pull her up in my lap just in time to hear the minister say, "And for our last hymn, turn to page eighty-seven, 'Let There Be Peace On Earth and Let It Begin In Me.'" And I'd quietly say, "Amen!"

As difficult as it was to get three little people to church (just to get to sing the closing song), somehow I always felt better. Maybe because I felt like this was part of the life I had chosen, and I was proud of myself for getting them there. Or could it have been that each Sunday I seemed to understand my mother and her prayer just a little bit more?

MOMMY CAN FIX IT

ONE AFTERNOON when Ashley was three years old, she was returning home from next door with her little red-haired girlfriend Bethie. As I watched them from the deck, I noticed Ashley had her hands cupped against her chest. Bethie was crying.

"Don't cry, Bethie, *my* Mommy can fix it," I overheard Ashley say comfortingly.

She walked up to me and uncupped her little hands, exposing a tiny baby rabbit that was obviously quite dead. She looked up at me with those big brown eyes and said, "Fix it, Mommy."

Slowly I took the little rabbit from her hands and tried to explain. I don't think I will ever forget the look on her face as she started to cry. We prepared a coffin out of an old Tupperware sandwich keeper, wrapped the little bunny in pink Kleenex, and gently placed it in the hole that we had dug in the back yard.

As I lifted the two little girls into my lap, I cried, too — not for the bunny, but because I realized there would be many tears shed by my beautiful child over things Mommy just couldn't fix.

A REAL DADDY

IN JULY 1983, my husband of nineteen years and I sat down with our three children to explain an upcoming event, our divorce. We kept saying the dumb things parents tell their children at a time like this . . . things like nothing's really going to change and everything is going to be just "fine."

We try making the unnatural seem natural, telling them Daddy will be living somewhere else, as if it should make them happy. Now they will have two rooms and two houses. We state these devastating facts like some cheery commercial, like two, two, mints in one.

After our announcement, their father hastily departed. The children and I were left seated on the couch silently huddled together. The boys, then nine and eleven, were unmoving, with tears streaming down their faces. Our daughter, barely five, fidgeted nervously and crawled in my lap.

Finally, the nine-year-old broke the silence asking if his dad left because he was so bad, voicing the first of endless questions they would ask as they groped to understand why. As time passed, their father dropped by for a trip to the movies, Chuck-E-Cheese, or the arcade. Each time they returned in varying moods and with unending questions. Sometimes they were visibly angry. Lance, after returning from one of these outings, glared at me saying, "You always tell me to do my best, Mom. Did you do your best?"

Then he stormed into his room, slamming the door. Standing in the hallway I could hear his crying. I was his mother; my job was to make his childhood safe and secure, but here I stood outside his door unable to make any more sense out of this than an eleven-year-old.

A few weeks later, their father called and said he would be picking up the boys but couldn't handle the little one this weekend. As I helped the boys with their packing, I explained to Ashley that this weekend was going to be special, just for us girls. After the boys left, we headed toward the movies, when all of a sudden she began shaking, screaming at me, "I hate you, I hate you, I hate you." I pulled the car off to the side of the road and tried to hold her. "I hate you," she continued. "You let my daddy leave, and now you let him take my brothers!"

I've heard it said that women in divorces are customarily "awarded" the children. Awarded, like they are inanimate objects to be won or lost. At this moment, I envied my ex-husband. He simply walked away to start a brand-new life. I was left to piece together this shattered mess, its enormity unbelievably magnified by three confused little people. For the first time in their lives, I was working full time. In a way they had lost both their parents.

A few days later I picked up Ashley at a playmate's. "Mommy," she began excitedly, "I know just how to fix everything. We get a long table . . . put candles in the middle . . . invite Daddy to dinner. You sit at one end and Daddy will sit at the other. I'll play slow music on my record player, then he will kiss you and come home."

MY GENERATION was the first in our family to experience divorce. My children received a stepmother and a stepfather, something they never asked for, an occurrence brought on by something broken.

Broken promises, broken vows causing broken hearts. They were forced, with no choice, to accept what they could not change, something that could never be mended — fragile feelings cracked beyond repair, dreams shattered like glass. And no matter how careful we are, we all bleed.

AFTER THE emergence of their daddy's new friend and subsequent marriage, the children realized their father and mother would never be together again. Each of them acted out their feelings in their own unique way. Lance, as the oldest, addressed me sternly saying, "You can get married again ,too, but not until I'm grown up and out of here because I am not going to live in a house with a stepfather."

My younger son seemed to sense the pain more than the others. "Don't worry, Mom," he said as he wound his arms around my neck. "You're so pretty someone else will love you." His thoughtfulness was short-lived and eventually erupted into anger. I was constantly at the principal's office. Courtney poured charcoal lighter on ant beds in the yard and set them on fire. He set off firecrackers in the kitchen.

My daughter, the eternal optimist, deduced the only way to return us to normalcy was to marry me off. This was a mission which this child attacked with unrelenting diligence. Every time we'd go out, her brown eyes scanned like radar for eligible suitors. Constantly she tugged at me, "Look at him, Mom, don't you think he is handsome?" Frustrated by my lack of enthusiasm, Ashley became bolder. She'd introduce herself to strange men, asking them if they were married, pointing at me, saying, "Don't you think my mom is pretty?"

When she invited the checkout clerk at the 7-Eleven to dinner, we had to talk. I was mortified. I was trying to explain that she was embarrassing me when I noticed tears streaming down her face. Defeatedly she whispered, "But Mom, I want a daddy."

"You already have a daddy," I reminded her.

"No, I don't!" she said. "I want a daddy who lives in the house with us and plays with me. I want a *real* daddy."

THE TOUCHABLES

EVERY TIME I was pregnant, I prayed as all mothers do for a healthy baby. I admit I felt guilty asking for more than that, but I also prayed that they would be loving and outgoing. I had seen so many little children hide behind their mothers' skirts, and I hated it. They seemed teased, shy and afraid. It was so sad to see little people with such wariness.

But my prayers were all answered. My gifts were three beautiful, healthy, outgoing and affectionate children. Nobody has ever said my three were shy or unaffectionate. These little ones were full of trust and love.

As they got older and I would stop by the high school, Lance would run up with a "Hi, Mom," sweeping me off my feet with a big bear hug. His younger brother, Courtney, would get upset about something and come into the kitchen and declare, "Mom, I need a hug." Until my daughter and I could no longer fit into the mauve stuffed rocker, she would say, "Mommy, rock me in the pink chair." These reminiscences are my very special treasures.

My children were touched, hugged, squeezed and even their

toes played with, as each little piggy went to market. I find it so sad to see a father and son greet each other after a long absence with a mature handshake. Adults accidentally touch one another and jump back saying, "Oh, excuse me." I hated having to warn the tiniest of human beings not to speak to strangers. Why can't they grow up believing strangers are friends they have yet to meet?

My children and I can't resist picking up a puppy and hugging it. Smelling its own unique smell. Same thing with babies. We see them and immediately want to squeeze them. I don't try to cultivate friendships with people who don't like puppies and babies. I know they are too mature, too grown-up, and much too sophisticated for me. They have forgotten the value in the tenderness of touching. They probably have never led with their hearts, only their very adult heads.

I admit my children and I have been hurt by offering the gift of acceptance and affection to some who didn't understand how precious it was. But to live and not to touch or be touched is not to live. I have watched people who were hurt wall themselves off to prevent their being hurt again. Yet they have also prevented themselves the chance of being loved. Now I am not an advocate of doling out movie star greetings, but squeeze those you love, hug your friends. Some will be taken back at first, but the majority are hug-starved.

We need to touch, hug and love each other. There are still some signs of gentleness and trust on this earth, like puppies and babies. We need to revert back to the wonderful child hidden in all of us. Hug a puppy, kiss a baby, get in touch with our disappearing tenderness. I pray that my children will remember my touch and see it as a legacy to pass on to their children and their children's children.

Yes Ma'am, No Ma'am,
Thank You Ma'am, Please

THE GENERATION I grew up with appears to be the last that was given clear rules and values. Maybe because they didn't work for us as we expected, we passed on a confused hodgepodge of messages that have given little or no foundation upon which our children can build. I remember being about five, lying on top of a wagon piled high with fresh-picked cotton, the sun shining down, all warm and safe, with my grandfather driving the tractor pulling us to the Northport gin.

As I lay there and watched the puffy cloud figures drift by in the blue Alabama sky, I knew who I was, where I came from, and what was expected of me. My life would be exciting, I would be something special, and Mother would be proud. She told me so. But this could only be achieved by following the rules. The rules were the Ten Commandments, which I could recite.

The rules also included subcategories. For example: under the fourth commandment, honor and respect, came not only your parents but also your elders, the law, the doctors, and all people in positions of authority. Respect was even extended to include animals. Animals were special because they taught basic responsibility. I don't know how old I was when I learned about the subcategories. It was as if I had always known.

Instinctively I knew to say, "Yes, ma'am; no, ma'am; thank you, ma'am; please." And if I had a momentary lapse in memory, my mother's right eyebrow would independently start to rise. If my manners escaped me until that eyebrow reached upward and stopped — I could cut my very own switch. It was even worse to be ill-mannered away from home because Mother would not further embarrass herself. I was required to wait for my punishment all the way home. She was consistent and she wouldn't forget. No matter how angelic I was on the drive home, it didn't change anything. I had earned it and I would get it — cause and effect.

I had and still have a conscience, and I truly believe I would have had a lot more fun without it. I'm not sure where I got it. The guilt, the fear, the control that this little voice could echo through my brain would send shock waves throughout my body when it whispered, "You'll get caught, you'll get hurt, they will be disappointed, you'll get a switching, they won't trust you anymore, you'll be sorry." And the conscience was usually right!

Even when I didn't get caught, the conscience tormented me. God knew, even if nobody else did. The welling guilt would eventually make me confess, if my little sister, Marie, didn't take care of it for me. I can still remember the form and the movement and the feeling of my switchings. My mother would extend her hand, and I would place mine in hers, knowing too well that I could depend on her not to let go until the punishment was complete. She would guide me along as I jumped up and down, hopping in a circle, screeching between sobs, "I'm sorry, I won't ever do it again!"

As I got older, I learned how to take the switchings less painfully and, I believe, not as lengthily. I learned, when my mother extended her hand to mine and I looked into those flaming green eyes, to meekly say, "Yes, ma'am." I did not speak during the switchings; *that* was the height of stupidity. If I said "I'm sorry" while she was switching me, she would have to repeat it, as she pumped the arm that held the switch that was needling my legs, "You better believe you're sorry. I taught you better. You knew, and you did it anyway. Don't tell me you're sorry. I know you're sorry and when I get through with you, you'll really be sorry!"

Now, while my mother elaborated and expounded on what *I* had said, the arm continuously pumped, giving her added momentum. I remember in one defiant moment, I put my hand in hers, our eyes met, and I said, with complete absence of mind, "You can whip me, but you can't make me cry." During the switching that followed, I never spoke but I commenced crying before her switch ever made contact with my legs.

There is an organization now called Tough Love, and the

members act like they thought up the concept. But I know better. My mother was the founder, and if she were still alive she would tell you so. My mother never read Dr. Spock, and I don't feel as if she were an abusive parent. She always said that a spanking hurt her a lot worse than it did me. This logic escaped me until I had children of my own. My children know where they came from, who they are, and I know that in their hearts they know right from wrong.

Unfortunately, I *did* read Dr. Spock, and I decided, after a time, to replace the whippings with "time-outs" and by withdrawing their privileges. Somewhere deep in my heart, I felt this was an error in judgment. My sons are grown now, but still they say things like, "Remember when we did (this or that childhood prank) and Mother used her switch on both of us at the same time?" They all laugh and remember what they did and the corporal punishment that I delivered. But you know, they never say, "Remember when Mom gave us a time-out?" But the switchings — they remained etched in their memories. I have often told them I felt that all our lives would have been easier if I hadn't stopped the switchings so soon.

My mother whipped my brother every Friday. She said he had to have it, that he wanted it terribly, and it was the only way that we could be assured of a pleasant weekend. She said that Mondays he would slowly begin to regress and by Fridays he would be begging for a whipping. I remember my mother apologizing one Saturday after my brother had aggravated everyone in the house and then proceeded to torment the dog in the yard. "I'm sorry for your brother's behavior. I was so busy Friday that I forgot his whipping." I am six years older than my brother and I love him dearly; but at age eleven, I remember I understood: he definitely needed his whippings if peace were to be had over the weekends. Mother would have a hard time understanding the children of today — how they could have been allowed to reach such a pinnacle of disrespect.

I remember an occasion when I was visiting my grandmother for a few days with my two young sons. She told me flatly, "These precious great-grandchildren will not get a switching at their granny's house." I said, "Yes, ma'am." Later that afternoon she came to me and said, "I'll cut the switch, and you switch 'em."

As parents, we work so hard these days to give our children what we think they should have and what they want, all the while denying them what they are silently begging for. The demise of our Southern heritage, the way we treat each other, the disrespect and lawlessness that are so rampant — I believe all this began when children stopped saying, "Yes, ma'am," and when mothers stopped giving their children a good whipping.

The Problem with Fred

MY DAUGHTER Ashley and I moved into an apartment when she was nine years old, after her older brothers went away to school. We missed them terribly. To compound our loneliness, we had to leave our dog behind because dogs were prohibited by our lease.

Near our apartment was a pet store, so many afternoons we stopped to visit the animals. One afternoon we were petting some puppies when we noticed a cage full of tiny long-eared rabbits. Ashley was thrilled. She opened the cage and gingerly lifted up what looked like a tiny black and white powder puff with long ears. As she nuzzled the little bunny, her big brown eyes lit up. "Oh, Mama, our lease didn't say we couldn't have a rabbit!" As I began to protest, she enlisted the help of the store manager who explained that with patience rabbits could be litter trained just like kittens.

Well, it took a *lot* of patience to litter train our new friend Fred, but we finally accomplished the task. Fred had quite a personality for a rabbit. He would stomp his foot when he became afraid or angry. And he would trip over his long ears when he ran. He was supposed to have been a dwarf rabbit but someone forgot to tell him. He looked like a very large black and white fuzzy cat except for the ears.

As he reached adulthood, his personality began to change. He began to make obscene advances to furniture legs. One evening he attached himself to Ashley's leg. I sat down trying to decide how to handle the subject when she said, "Mother, what is Fred doing?"

Searching for the right words, I said, "You remember in *Bambi* how Thumper got all twitterpated when he saw the female rabbit?"

Ashley jerked Fred from her leg. "You mean Fred thinks my leg is a female rabbit?"

"Well," I said, "Fred has grown up with just you and me and he's probably very confused."

Later that same evening Fred was up to another trick — grabbing things and running. I popped him with a dish towel and said, "Quit it, Fred!" Ashley came running to his defense, admonishing me. "Mother, how can you fuss at Fred? You know he's under a lot of stress!"

Fred's problem grew worse. He would hide behind the front door and attach himself to anyone who entered.

My sister dropped in one afternoon. Fred pounced. From the kitchen I could see she was hopping around in a circle, trying to kick Fred off her leg and screaming, "If you don't get rid of this crazy rabbit, I'm not ever coming over here again!"

The pizza delivery boy proved to be the pivotal point in our life with Fred. When the pizza boy walked in, Fred pounced and the pizza went flying.

As we scraped cheese off the top of the pizza box, Ashley handed Fred a piece of pepperoni. "Mom, Fred needs a female rabbit." I agreed, but implored her to understand that would be the beginning of something the apartment management absolutely would not condone. We would have to find Fred a new home with creatures of his own kind.

That next Saturday, Ashley, Fred, and I drove sixty miles to a petting zoo in Tuscaloosa. Ashley walked up and down the cages of female rabbits and finally stopped at the cage of a fuzzy brown lady rabbit, with a big white spot on her head. She held Fred up and the rabbits' noses met. "This is the one," she said, as the owner opened the cage and Fred hopped inside.

I was afraid Ashley might get upset or start to cry about leaving Fred, but she seemed very pleased with herself. As we walked to the car she slipped her hand in mine and grinned.

"Do you think when we get home we could order pizza?"

Mom Boyd's Pew

W HEN THE backwoods of Alabama were sparsely inhabited, the old clapboard churches were the hub of social and religious gatherings. My direct ancestors have been ministers, elders, and deacons at Liberty Church on Bear Creek since November 14, 1835, when it received its charter. My grandmother, Willie Avery Lewis, was one of the first lady delegates to the Tuscaloosa Baptist Association after the suffrage amendment in 1920.

As was the custom in many of the country churches, Mother's Day was homecoming, with an all-day singing and dinner on the ground. On Mother's Day, my Grannie Willie and my great-grandmother, "Mom Boyd," would bring roses, bridal wreath, and forsythia to place on family graves. They would have been baking for days, and the aroma of their craft would fill our '53 Chevy.

We didn't go to Liberty every Sunday, but on Mother's Day it would have seemed unnatural not to be there. It was like a call that went out to the brothers and sisters of old Liberty, and no matter how far from Duncanville they had ventured, on Mother's Day they came home.

Mothers wore white corsages signifying their mothers had passed on, and we wore our red rosebud corsages, meaning we still had our moms. The oldest and newest mothers in the church would be recognized and applauded. Mothers were special, and that day the celebration was in their honor.

I had not the foggiest idea who the relatives were that pinched my cheeks, patted my head, hugged, and kissed me. I would hear my name and Mom Boyd would say, "This is my great-granddaughter." An elderly lady would then pat, pinch, or hug, saying, "Why, you're the spittin' image of your great-grandmother."

Then Grandmother would be calling, and she'd say, "This is Grace's daughter." The person I was being shown to this time would say, "I haven't seen you since you were just a little bitty thing. You're just as pretty as your grandmother!" I'd lower my eyes and say, "Thank you, ma'am," waiting a respectful moment before I would tear down the hill to continue catching the big black and orange grasshoppers that hid among the tombstones. About that time Mother would call. She'd want me to meet some cousins I didn't even know I had, and they said, "Well, Mary Jean, you look just like your mother did when she was your age."

I never got angry with all the interruption to my playing because the same thing was happening to all the other children, too. It was Mother's "Brag Day," but not bragging in a bad way. They were very proud of their children and their families. It was sort of like when one of the old people touched you, today and tomorrow were joined in an orderly fashion with yesterday. I felt sorry for my dad—his mother and father were dead, and his people were still in Hungary. He had no one to show us off to.

Some time during the day my granddaddy and I would take a walk through the cemetery, and he'd introduce me to all the people there. It didn't seem sad or spooky; it was just a special place for our family members who had gone on before us.

By the time Mother started rounding us up and searching for shoes, we would be stuffed and happily exhausted. Usually we fell asleep in the car on the way home.

In 1958 I was eleven. We had a '56 two-tone green Plymouth station wagon. Dad and Granddaddy were coming down later. Mother was driving, and my little brother was up front in Grandmother's lap as usual. My sister and I sat in the back seat with our great-grandmother. "Mom Boyd," I said, "when I have a baby, there'll be five generations of us going to Liberty."

"Oh no," she said in a half laugh. "I'm hoping I won't be here that long!" Shocked by the thought of her not being with us, I said, "What do you mean?"

"Because," she said, "I'm eighty-two years old. I've outlived two husbands, most of my friends, and these old bones are tired." I felt very sad the rest of the drive. I guess I realized Mom Boyd would never see my children or brag on them on Mother's Day.

The next year, as always, we went back to Liberty on Mother's Day. We had one more grave to visit, one more to decorate: Mom Boyd's.

AFTER MY SONS left home in 1987, my daughter and I moved back to Alabama. We were getting ready to go to our new church in Birmingham that first Mother's Day when I heard it, the call of old Liberty. I realized my daughter was nine years old and had never lived in Alabama or been to Liberty.

We went to Tuscaloosa and turned down on Highway 82 to Duncanville and up the dirt road. A new brick church stood in the place of the old house. The oak trees were still there, only much larger, and a long line of tables waited in the shade for dinner to be spread. My daughter followed me inside. At first all the newness seemed so strange. Then I noticed it; there on the left-hand side on the front of one of the pews was a little brass plaque that read, "In loving memory of John Samuel and Mary Jane Boyd."

After a few hymns Brother Tatum came up to the pulpit and began preaching on footprints in the sands of time, and how if we as Christians simply sat while God's laws were broken, we would leave a very different imprint.

My daughter leaned over and whispered, "Why is he so red in the face and talking so loud?" I smiled and patted her leg. "He just wants to make sure you hear him, and that you realize he means what he says."

As we left the church, Brother Tatum was greeting everyone. He had become pastor at Liberty when I was three years old in 1948. He looked at me for a minute and said, "I don't know which one you are, but you're one of Aunt Willie's grandchildren."

"I'm Mary Jean." Putting my arm around my daughter's shoulders, I said, "This is my daughter, Ashley Grace." He looked from my brown eyes to hers and said, "You're just as pretty as your mother." She smiled and said, "Thank you."

I took her by the hand and led her down into the cemetery so I could introduce her. The graves of Papa and Mom Boyd were on the left as we entered. I stopped and remembered a little rhyme Mom Boyd taught me in Cherokee and repeated it.

I went back to Liberty this year with my daughter and my oldest son. I didn't recognize as many faces, and the food wasn't quite as good as I remembered. But miraculously, Old Brother Tatum's still there. It is not a sad place, even though I wear a white corsage. The children and I turned to page seventy-seven in the blue Broadman hymnal and began singing "The Old Rugged Cross." I could only hope . . . that one day my children find the sense of peace and belonging somewhere, as I have, right there in Mom Boyd's pew.

IT'S HARD TO DRIVE WITH
UNCLE LOMAN IN THE TRUNK

S HE DIDN'T ASK where we were going. She just took my arm and walked with me to the car. She trusted me. After all, I was the only one she had left. Her children and her husband had died, and here I was, the oldest grandchild, taking her to Merry Wood Lodge Nursing Home. She and my grandfather had shared their house for sixty-seven years, and I had sold it. It was the last time she would walk from her home down those kitchen steps.

Looking at the giant pecan trees and the fig tree my great-grandfather had planted, my heart ached with the realization of what I was doing. The big old house had become imbued with sights and sounds only Grandmother heard. The people who once lived there filled her nights and days with confusion and torment. A sadness would surround her as she stared around, trying to find matches to light the electric stove to fix dinner for her disappearing loved ones. She would walk down the highway searching in vain, calling out their names.

I consoled myself, repeating over and over again silently,

Uncle Loman

"This is for her own good." But as we started the seventy-five mile drive to the nursing home near my house, nothing about it seemed good. She stared out the window and pointed at anything that caught her attention. Finally she looked over and asked the question I had dreaded so terribly. "Where are we going?"

I took a deep breath and tightened my grip on the steering wheel and prayed that the right words would come to me. "I'm taking you to live near us, Grandmother. You live so far away we don't get to see you as often as we'd like."

She said nothing and continued to look out the window like a curious child. Further down the road she looked over at me and said, "I know where we're going."

"You do?" I said.

"Yes, we're going to bury Loman."

"Oh, no, Grandmother, Uncle Loman's not dead."

"He's back there." She pointed toward the trunk.

Uncle Loman is Grandmother's baby brother. He's in his seventies and has Alzheimer's, too, but he was alive and definitely not in my trunk. I tried repeatedly to reassure her.

She would only be quiet for a few moments, then start the same train of thought all over again. "Is this the exit to the cemetery? Did you order flowers? When did he die?" On and on I drove. Seventy-five miles seemed like seven hundred fifty miles. Mile markers got farther and farther apart. I tried to remind her how we had taken Uncle Loman some of the ice cream sandwiches that he dearly loved only the week before. Didn't she remember?

"No, Grandmother, I don't know what cemetery that is to our left. No, Grandmother, I haven't missed the exit."

Please don't let her become hysterical or cry and please, God, don't let *me* cry. By now I was chain smoking, wondering if I was going to spend eternity driving down Interstate 65. I wondered if the trip would ever end, and I was terrified by the uncertainty that lay ahead. I couldn't go back, I couldn't stop, and I dreaded going forward.

"Did you mean to turn there? How much further is the cemetery?"

I wanted to agree with her but I couldn't, she was so confused. Her oldest daughter, my Aunt Lou, had just died with cancer, and my mom was long dead of a car accident, and Grandmother's husband, Papa Troy, had died at eighty-nine of heart failure. Even her only sister was gone, and that left just me and Uncle Loman.

At last, our exit appeared. We made the turnoff on Highway 14, and I remembered we had to drive right past a very large cemetery. When we approached it, she looked over at me. I just shook my head and stared straight ahead. By now I had said silent prayers to every saint and angel I had ever heard of.

"Grandmother, I wouldn't lie to you. Uncle Loman's not dead."

"What about Troy?" she asked.

"Yes, Grandmother, Granddaddy's been gone a long time."

We came up a circular drive to the front of the nursing home, but there was no sigh of relief for me. I felt like I could hardly breathe, as if all the air around me was suddenly disappearing. If I couldn't make her understand that Uncle Loman wasn't in the trunk, *how* was I going to make her understand all this? A pleasant looking lady came rushing out the front door of the nursing home and opened Grandmother's car door. She said in a sweet voice, "You must be Mrs. Fikes. Welcome to your new home, we've been waiting for you."

"Well, thank you," said Grandmother. She held out her walker and, with all the dignity of her eighty-seven years, she walked inside. I heard myself rattling on about how the children and I would see her often, and I would call her every day. Then she stopped, looked up at me with that sweet face, and said, "Troy's not here, is he?"

"No, Grandmother."

She paused and then said quietly, "Do you think Loman might come?"

I put my arms around her and whispered, "I hope so, Grandmother. I hope so."

PULLEY BONES

SUNDAYS WERE always family days in our home. As I've gotten older, the family seems to have gotten smaller each year: deaths, divorces, and distances take their relentless toll.

One lovely Sunday in September, the need to be around loved ones came up with the sun. So, off we went to Merry Wood to spring Grannie Willie. My second husband, my daughter, stepson and I headed down Highway 9 to the Hotel Talisi, known for its home cooking and the player piano in the lobby. We filed into the old dining room and seated Grannie Willie at the head of the table. As I folded her walker, she instructed me as to what to bring her from the buffet table. Plate in hand, I began to sort through the mound of golden fried chicken for a small piece. There, snuggled down between a leg and wing, I saw it — a pulley bone.

I placed it on Grandmother's plate next to the watermelon rind preserves. When I returned to the table, I announced proudly to my crew, "Look, I found a pulley bone!" They looked at me with puzzled faces, as they so often do. "This piece of chicken," I said. "They don't cut up chicken like this anymore. It's a separate piece, a pulley bone." Then I sat back and thought, as they stared at me, how stupid it must seem for a forty-five-year-old woman to be so excited about a piece of chicken. And what made me call it a pulley bone?

Instead of privately enjoying my find, I felt compelled to explain to them that a pulley bone was next to the breast on the chicken, and the person who was fortunate enough to get this special piece could, after removing all the meat, ask anyone at the table to help pull the bone apart. Whoever got the small piece of the bone would be married first, while the longest piece signified good luck. As a child, I thought either prediction was wonderful. My daughter, quite the lady at thirteen, said, "Mother, don't you mean the wishbone?" My husband and stepson proceeded with their meal, and Grandmother smiled.

When she finished eating the meat from the little piece of chicken, she handed it to my daughter who, deciding to humor us, took it and offered it to her stepbrother. He, good sport that he is, helped her pull it apart. I was so happy that Brian got the piece that promised an early marriage, leaving my Ashley the good luck piece. After all, she was the youngest and the last to keep me from the "empty nest syndrome." She looked so pretty, her skin so tanned, her eyes such a bright brown, and her body showing the signs of impending womanhood. I felt tears start to well up in my eyes, and I fought to retain my composure.

Suddenly there was a barrage of memories. Sights and sounds seemed to pound through my body. I excused myself and headed for the ladies' room, not wanting to flub through an explanation of why a piece of chicken bone in my daughter's hand had suddenly brought me to tears.

My God, I thought, I remember and miss so much of times gone by. I miss the chinaberries with which my brother and I waged war and my sister made necklaces. I miss porch swings and making pine straw playhouses. I miss running barefoot through red-topped clover. I miss skipping and being able to do backbends and splits. I miss not having to lock our doors at night. I miss sleeping near the fireplace with clothesline-dried blankets piled high. I miss hearing, "Yes, ma'am," "no, ma'am," "Thank you, ma'am," and "Please." I miss homegrown tomatoes and yard eggs. I miss the roosters' crowing to signal the beginning of a new day. I miss picnics at the spring and clear water in the pond. I miss eating chocolate cake and being thin. I miss playing hide-and-seek and my dog, Teddy. I miss the feel of my baby's cheeks so soft next to mine. I miss Mom Boyd, Papa Troy and Aunt Lou.

But most of all, Mother, I just miss pulley bones and you.

PAINTING PICTURES

*T*HANKSGIVING and Christmas dinners bring such expectation. It's as if we believe they will be like a Currier and Ives painting, "Father Knows Best" or "The Waltons." We eat those lovely meals riddled with not so lovely thoughts. We expect everything to be *so* perfect, all the while sabotaging any hope of its being so.

Usually the designated hostess, an older sister, mom or grandmother, is so exhausted she can barely eat by the time the meal is served. A few relatives bring dishes only they like. Others bring dishes they don't even like just because they always have. Every year someone brings this stupid red Jell-O with fruit cocktail, marshmallows, and pecans, and nobody eats it.

One relative usually shows up out of obligation and guilt, bringing a guest who is in a state of shock from all the confusion. Someone is always depressed because she wasn't invited anywhere else. One mother's upset because her son had to go with his wife to her family for dinner. A place is vacant one year, and the next year a high chair is added to the other end of the table.

The teenagers hate giving up their T-shirts and places to go. Someone spills a drink on the lace tablecloth, and a child gets a whipping. Another youngster gets the giggles and is sent from the table. And the husbands are furious because they can't see the football game on TV from the dining room. The wives are just dreading the dishes.

But me, I love it all. This *is* a family. I just wish someone would paint it the way it really is.

A SHORT PITY PARTY

*L*IFE—that continuous span of time spent becoming disenchanted, disillusioned, disheartened, discarded, and discussed. All my life I've been accused of being the eternal optimist. Am I just beat up, beat down, tired, or maybe sick?

I'm forty-seven today. Happy Birthday! This feels like the second coming of teenage confusions and frustrations. Same set of problems, just more involved and more of them. Same conflicts between right and wrong, fair and unfair. Except now they have labels: depression, fatigue syndrome, and dependent personalities. At age seventeen, they said it was hormonal and at forty-seven they say it may be hormonal. I've decided *life* is *definitely* hormonal.

I wish, as I look out this window, my life could be more like my geraniums. They grow green and strong and full blossomed. I provide them with tender loving care by cutting off dead leaves so new ones will grow. I give them water, sunlight, and fertilizer so they have everything they need. I cover them from the elements to prevent damage and death. People notice their vibrant red blooms and smile because they can see that they are loved. My geraniums don't ask me to take care of them. I want to!

Sometimes I feel like life should be that simple. I wonder if I stopped worrying and running around and just sat on the porch by the geraniums, would someone come by and take care of *me*?

'C' FOR ME

THE LITTLE GIRL looked up at me with big blue eyes, pointed, and asked softly, "What happened to your arm?" I turned on her without hesitation. "It was a shark attack," I said. "It got the person next to me and was only able to bite off the top of my shoulder."

"Oh," she said, her eyes much wider now. I watched her walk away, staring out into the ocean. Why did I say that? Why couldn't I just say, "I had cancer." Maybe she wouldn't have even understood, but, as she looked out into the waves, it was obvious she did know what sharks were. God, I am so mean. I've even stooped to scaring little children. How could she know this was the first time I had put my arm on public display. It had been so hard to take off my beach coat.

I sat for a long time listening to the waves as they chastised me saying, "You are still alive."

No matter how much sense the waves made, I just sat there feeling sorry for myself. I was angry. Four operations, just on that ugly, pink-scarred arm. Then, all of a sudden, I began to laugh.

The plastic surgeon had taken three inches out of my stomach to make me a new shoulder, and a skin graft off my right hip. No wonder I had said what I did to the little girl. No wonder I was so angry and mean. I was probably the only person in the world who could say, "I've got my ass on my shoulder," and literally be telling the truth!

POPSICLE CROSSES

THERE IS ONLY one thought on my mind this morning. This day, July 5, 1991, is the last day of a child's life.

I keep going over in my mind the events of the last few weeks, wondering why nothing — why no one — can stop this.

At 8:30 in the morning a baby will die, my son's child and my first grandchild. I know that my son's girlfriend will regret this for the rest of her life, but that is no comfort.

I close my eyes and all I can see is a tiny baby with little fingers and toes, its little heart already beating, all snug and warm in its mother's womb. I am thankful that at least it doesn't know.

She told me it was her baby, her body, and she had the legal right to make this decision. And I know she is stating facts. But this baby is already a part of our families.

The girlfriend's little sister and my daughter are the same age, and they keep begging us to stop this. My son's girlfriend says they are only fourteen and can't possibly understand. But the wisdom of children sometimes transcends age. And to them, abortion — and all acts that cause pain and death — are wrong.

Isn't that what we taught them? Where does this innocent justice, this profound sense of right and wrong, go? At what age do the commandments no longer apply? When do these laws change to suite our own selfish lives?

She didn't refer to the little life as an embryo or fetus. She called it "the baby." I don't understand. A baby is a little person who looks to its mother for care and protection. Helpless, it sleeps in her womb until tomorrow. Tears run constantly from my eyes, and I can't stop them either. This precious baby would have brought happiness to our family. A new reason for sharing ourselves and our love. Instead, we are faced with the loss of a loved one that will be deprived of not only its life, but also of being a part of our lives. I've tried not to dwell on it, but I can't help wondering if it's a boy or girl. What color eyes does it have? Does it look like my son?

I think of my children when they were babies and the beautiful journey we traveled as I watched them discover the world around them. Seeing their wonder and innocence, I redis-covered the world anew through their eyes.

She says she doesn't want the responsibility. I pleaded with her to see this child as a blessing she could give to a childless couple. But she tells me she does not want to lose her figure. For this reason, a child must die.

My children, no matter how much trouble they've been, are a wonderful gift that I cherish. The major part of my life's work has been to provide a home for them filled with life-living, growing things. We've planted vegetable gardens, flowers, and trees. They had a puppy that grew up and had puppies, seven of them so terribly ugly that everyone who saw them laughed and wanted one. We had thousands of guppies and other fish. Birds with broken wings, two finches named Jack and Diane, and a white rabbit named Pooka. We had a black cocker spaniel named Snow White and an unruly newt named Norman. All of these things were part of the celebration we call life.

I'm not saying our home was perfect. But throughout our trials, there was always love, laughter, and living. When our pets passed on, we had funerals in the yard with Tupperware coffins and Popsicle crosses with the animals' names painted on them.

I have always been against abortion, especially as a means of birth control. Now that it touches my life personally, it is even more horrible than I imagined. Tomorrow morning will bring a great sadness into my life, different from any sadness I have ever known. How could I be prepared for this? My mother wouldn't have understood any more than I do.

In January, I would have held my first grandchild. Instead, in the morning a part of me will be pulled apart as this baby is dismembered. I cry and the pain and sadness of tomorrow will forever be a part of our family. For my son's child, my first grandchild, there will be no funeral, not even a Popsicle cross to prove that it did, indeed, once exist.

THE LADY OF THE LAKE

WHEN MY Grandfather bought his farm in Tuscaloosa County, there was an old dilapidated store barely standing on one corner of the property. As they were clearing the store away, they found a picture in a back room under some tin. Granddaddy wiped it off. Then he hung it in the little parlor off his dining room. It was a print signed by a woman named Zula Kenyton. A sixteen by twenty inch picture that depicts a very feminine lady with her chin resting gently on her hands, as she sits alone in a row boat. The oars rest peacefully on the water. She gazes out, as if in deep thought. The moon's reflection over her shoulder makes a path toward her. The picture's only color is her dress, a soft, muted pink.

When my daughter, Ashley, was born in 1977, Granddaddy took the picture off the wall and handed it to me. I was thrilled because I'd always loved that picture. "Why are you giving it to me now?" I asked. He said, "Because, I hope she," referring to Ashley, "runs you as crazy as you did me about it." Seeing my confusion, he continued, "When you were just a little thing you would hold your arms up pointing to the picture saying, 'Hold me up Papa so I can see the lady.' Then you would proceed with a litany of questions about her. 'Papa, why is her by herself? Where is her momma? Is her scared? Is her lost?'" He said he'd hold me up until his arms began to ache and become numb.

It's been over eighteen years since he gave me the picture. Only now Papa's not here to hold me up or give me the answers.

Although the lady and I have moved many times, her picture still hangs in my hallway. Five years ago, we moved into an old house out on Lake Jordan in Alabama. With my children old enough to stand on their own, I find myself with time to think. As I look out past her across the water, I sometimes feel I have become the lady in the picture. I hear a little voice from deep inside me.

Why is her by herself? Where is her momma? Is her scared? Is her lost?

THE CEMETERY

FOR SOME REASON I noticed an old man at the red light turning into the cemetery. Maybe it was the look on his face or maybe I'm just naturally curious, but I pulled over to the side of the road and watched him as he eased the beat-up blue Ford to a halt.

He got out and stood momentarily straight, as if to gather himself. In his hand he carried a branch of fuchsia crepe myrtle. He walked around the tombstones on a path obviously familiar to him. He stopped and slowly removed his hat. Then he tenderly lay the flower on the ground before him. His lips began moving. I could only imagine his words. A few minutes passed, he wiped his eyes with the back of his hand, not replacing his hat until he reached the car. He glanced back and then drove away.

I had felt a strong urge to go over and put my arms around him. I had wanted him to know he wasn't alone and, because of my own losses, I also felt his sadness. I couldn't help but wonder if the object of his affection had known the depth of his love prior to her death, or if it was only in death that she was truly loved.

THE NAME GAME

BOTH MY maternal great-grandmothers were named Mary Jane. I always wished that had been my name, instead of Mary Jean.

My parents named me Jean, not for who I was, but for what I wasn't. My father's name was Edward Eugene Fielder, and he had desperately wanted a son. I suppose it might have been worse. They could have named me Edwina Eugenia. My last name, Fielder, wasn't even our *real* name. My Grandfather Eugene *Fiedler* was from Hungary. To escape the prejudice of the time, he Americanized *Fiedler* by rearranging the letters into *Fielder*. Maybe it sounded better to him, since he had a Hungarian accent, but if I had been a boy, I would have reclaimed my *real* last name.

I played a lot of softball when I was young and always wanted to be pitcher or shortstop because it sounded so redundantly stupid hearing, "Fielder in the outfield."

I'd make up new names for myself all the time and told Mother when I got grown and had enough money, I was going to get myself a new name. Some girls had really neat nicknames, but besides being called Mean Mary Jean, I was called Bean Pole, Little Eddie, Cottontop, and Stinky. I wanted a pretty name, a real girl's name. My first name was Mary, but it somehow didn't suit me. Mary had a religious connotation, especially by itself, and Mean Mary Jean didn't seem holy (or heaven-sent).

In the first grade I met a girl named Happy Hinton. I really liked that. It had a wonderful sound: Happy Hinton. So I decided to work with the same letters for my first and last names, searching for an alliteration that sounded like Happy's. Fredia, Francis, and Fanny were all I could come up with. It seemed hopeless.

When I grew up, marriage provided a new name. My first husband's name was Jerry Wayne Etheridge. Now, I do love the South; however, Mary Jean and Jerry Wayne made it sound like there were a lot more than just the two of us. My second husband's name was Ensley. That wasn't much better, and I was stuck with the same initials. I wished I had married someone with a last name that started with a B. Then I would have simplified the whole thing by just being J. B.

I console myself by thinking of my poor grandmother. Her name was Willie: Willie Avery Lewis, after her deceased father, William Avery Lewis. She also was named for what she wasn't.

But my mother should have known better! She hated her first name and never told anybody what it was. It was Nellie, Nellie Grace Fikes. She said she asked Granddaddy one day why she was named Nellie, and he said he named her after a cow he once had. My mother was named after a cow! My imagination ran wild as I thought of what she could have named me if she had made this a family tradition.

I mentioned my name problem to my daughter one day, and she said, "Mom, you're a blonde. It *could* be worse. They could have named you Bambi or Candie or Crissie."

Now my first husband gave me pet names, stupid pet names like "Pumpie" instead of "Pumpkin" and "Honeybun." Cute, maybe, but not very creative. My second husband was worse. He couldn't remember my name. He called me by *other* women's names.

I now have, including my maiden name, three last names to choose from and I don't want any of them, but I think my self-esteem might suffer if I went simply by "Hey, you."

With women's lib and sexual harassment, the names I did like are now considered derogatory. I much preferred being called "Sweetheart" or "Honey" to "Mean Mary Jean."

Shakespeare wrote, "What's in a name? That which we call a rose by any other name would smell as sweet." It's pretty obvious nobody ever called William Shakespeare "Mean Mary Jean."

About the Author

Mary Jean Fielder was born in Tuscaloosa, Alabama. She has two sons, Lance and Courtney, and one daughter, Ashley, and recently added to the list her first grandchild, Peyton. In addition to the experiences recounted in *Mean Mary Jean*, she has worked as a nurse, a marketing director, a movie extra, and most importantly as a single mom. She now lives with her husband in Houston, Texas.